The Urban
Knitter

LILY M. CHIN

The Urban Knitter

BERKLEY BOOKS, NEW YORK

ℝ

A Berkley Book
Published by The Berkley Publishing Group
A division of Penguin Putnam Inc.
375 Hudson Street
New York, New York 10014

Copyright © 2002 by Lily M. Chin
Book design by Tiffany Kukec
Cover design by Erika Fusari
Cover and insert photographs by Alec Hemer

PRINTING HISTORY
Berkley trade paperback edition / February 2002

Visit our website at
www.penguinputnam.com

Library of Congress Cataloguing-in-Publication Data

Chin, Lily M.
        The urban knitter / Lily M. Chin.
            p. cm.
        Includes bibliographical references.
        ISBN 0-425-18328-9
        1. Knitting—Patterns. I. Title.

    TT820 .C48493 2002
    746.43'2041—dc21
                        2001052777

PRINTED IN THE UNITED STATES OF AMERICA

10 9 8 7 6 5 4

Contents

Acknowledgments

I dedicate this book to my devoted husband and best friend and sometimes-editor, Clifford Pearson. He cooks for me and consoles me. He puts up with me and that says a lot! Most importantly, he loves me and I love him.

Many thanks to Lisa Considine who sought me out to do this book. Thanks also go to Rick Mondragon and Cheryl Kellman for their tireless support and encouragement.

Of course, gratitude is expressed to those yarn companies and suppliers for providing our materials. I must not forget Andrea Monfried for consultation and advice throughout two books now. Special thanks to photographer Alec Hemer for coming through. Lastly, thanks to our Hip, Young, Urban Knitters, whom I fondly refer to as HYUKs. Without their talent, perseverance, and cooperation, this book would not have been possible.

Special thanks to Ann Regis, for wonderfully sensitive technical consultation.

Introduction

Don't knit. Only grannies knit. Knitting is for those with too much time on their hands. Knit if you don't have anything better to do.

This attitude has been all too pervasive for some time. However, let me introduce you to some *real* knitters I know. There's a financial analyst in Miami who has two young children, yet she manages to juggle family, career, and knitting. There's a linguistics professor in Los Angeles who is working on a description of knitting patterns using phonological theory for her web page. Then there's the trademark paralegal in Oakland who works to support his two-skeins-a-day knitting habit. Do these sound like stereotypes?

■

Knitting has been around for a long time. Knitted socks were found in the ancient tombs of Egypt. Before the advent of mass production and knitting machines, hand knitting produced necessities like socks and underwear, and the knitter was likely to be a man.

After the industrial revolution, though, knitting was primarily relegated to the home. It took on domestic implications as wives, mothers, and daughters knitted to clothe their families in warm woollies.

In modern society knitting is mostly a pastime,

a hobby rather than a necessity. For decades it has suffered from an association with dowdiness. Knitting seemed tied to the stereotypical granny image that such domesticity implied. (Of course, we can politicize the suggestions of undervalued women's work.)

Change is now under way, however. Knitting is appealing to more and more people, younger folk in particular. Men are picking it up again as they had done in the distant past. Those from all walks of life are discovering the esthetic, practical, and therapeutic benefits knitting has to offer.

For years, I felt like quite an anomaly. As a young person who knitted, it was difficult to find companions who shared my interests. I found very few knitters in my native New York City in the under-forty set. Though I had knitted since my adolescent years and had no intention of giving it up, I found it a solitary activity.

Then things began to change. I started noticing fellow knitters on the subways. At fittings for fashion runway shows, the models began to turn up with yarn and needles in hand. Internet groups for and about knitting were springing up like weeds. Guilds were forming. Even as I type, my book editor, Susan Allison, has completed yet another sweater for herself as well as a vest for her husband as she nurses a broken kneecap. Many others at the offices of Penguin Putnam knit as

well. At last, knitting, which was now my vocation, had become a hot thing to do.

Why was this happening all of a sudden? I'm sure the reports of role-model celebrities such as Julia Roberts, Cameron Diaz, Wynona Ryder, Daryl Hannah, and even Monica Lewinsky picking up the needles contributed to the direction knitting was taking. They made knitting a glamorous and "in" thing to do. Martha Stewart featured knitting in both her magazine and her television show. Other popular media were picking up on the trend and running with it. As a matter of fact, I was featured on a CNN news segment as well as numerous periodicals, such as *Time* magazine, for my knitting.

Perhaps the general public collectively discovered the many advantages of knitting. We can satisfy creative urges, fill in downtime efficiently, and soothe our souls. Indeed, many scientific studies have found knitting to be a relaxing way to decompress. With today's hectic pace we need to "chill," and knitting, like a form of meditation or yoga, serves as a means to do that. Furthermore, there is a marvelous end product to enjoy. And knitting is forgiving—where else in life is it possible to simply rip out mistakes and start over?

Pick up any of the many newspaper articles or magazine stories that feature knitting and see how others account for the phenomenon. I've seen it explained as an "antidote to high-tech" and a "backlash to mousing around in the computer age." How ironic then that computers would provide the glue that tied together everyone involved with the creation of this book!

Whatever the reason, I relate to this new audience for knitting. I know all too well the difficulties in finding patterns that appeal to the twenty- and thirty-something knitters. Because I want to inspire and encourage this next wave of fiberists, and because I wish to dispel that old and dowdy misconception of what a knitter is like, I created *The Urban Knitter*. It speaks to this new audience in its own voice.

How This Book Came About

From the beginning, my idea was to profile young, urban knitters in cities across the country. I fondly refer to them as Hip, Young, Urban Knitters, or HYUKs. Finding them was not a problem. Messages spread across the Internet and many responses followed.

I looked for knitters of every gender, race, ethnicity, religion, orientation . . . I wanted to showcase the full range and diversity of knitters out there. I also wanted several levels of ability and experience. My only criteria were that they live within city limits and that they be under forty. I wanted to present the fresh, new face of knitting.

Through the magic of the Internet, we became a group. Cher in Chicago set up a private mailing list for the twenty members, so that we could share files and photos readily.

Each HYUK then described the kind of project he or she wanted to work on. What kinds of things were these HYUKs interested in making? Many wanted hip garments and accessories that, as middle-income earners, they can't afford to buy in boutiques. Others sought interesting techniques to help hone their skills. Then there were those who were interested in simpler projects to fit within very busy schedules. Very often, the projects turned out to be all these things at once! I found the same wide range in projects as I did in HYUKs.

My role was to help the others realize their design ideas. Many knitters knew what they wanted to knit but did not necessarily have all the skills needed to bring their concepts to fruition. Others lacked the time. Still others lacked confidence. That's where I came in, to aid in the realization of the ideas, to translate the HYUK needs into design terms. I also matched them up with yarn.

A few of these talented HYUKs required very little help or input from me. Tara took off on her own and just needed fine-tuning with the directions for her sweater. Kie did just about every thing for her shoes from start to finish. Catherine worked out most of her socks by herself. Ingrid did her purse with nary a peep from me. Tony only needed initial suggestions and guidance with his vest. Daniel also worked out his accessories independently.

Thus, these are stories about knitters and their knitting visions. They are about a process. We will guide you every step of the way if you want to journey down the same road. It is my wish that readers will perhaps recognize themselves in these stories of knitters and projects. I hope that we will inspire them to pick up the needles and join our growing ranks.

Conventions

This book assumes that you know how to knit. There may be references to certain techniques such as mattress seaming or the slip-slip-knit decrease ([slip next st as if to knit] twice, insert the left-hand needle from left to right through the fronts of these 2 sts, then knit the two together in this position [through their back loops]). While I've included details of certain methods, if a term or technique is not familiar to you I urge you to look it up in one of the many references and resources that are found in the back of the book. In order to be understood by relatively new knitters, I have limited those abbreviations standard to the industry to a bare minimum. I have tried to write instructions in plain English.

By and large, the only abbreviations I've used throughout are:

k = knit
p = purl
st(s) = stitch(es)

Occasionally, you may also find RS for Right Side (the side that is meant to be seen) and WS for Wrong Side (the side that may be hidden). There will also be the infrequent C4B, or cable 4 back, but this and any others will be explained in the text of the directions first. Unless there is a specific type of increase called for, use one you are familiar with or one of your own choosing.

If there are several sizes, the smallest size is given first and each subsequent size is given in order within the parentheses. If there is only one number, it applies to all sizes.

Choose your size well. Look at the finished measurements. Know your own measurements. Think about how you like your clothes to fit. Usually, a garment is a few inches larger than your largest measurement, very often the bust or chest. The way a garment fits is determined by how much bigger the garment is than you are. Fewer inches will result in a closer fit. Many more inches create a looser fit. It sometimes helps to measure a garment you already own to see how big a size you are aiming for.

View the garment's schematic measurements and compare them to your own. Measurements such as body length are easily adjustable. (Of course, adding more length will require a bit more yarn.)

Other measurements such as sleeve length are more involved and will require personal adaptation. You may have to alter the "rate" at which you add the stitches that widen the sleeve. For instance, if you lengthen the sleeve, instead of increasing every 4th row every so often, you would increase every 6th row a few times instead.

Chart reading may be new to some readers. In essence, each stitch and row is represented. Horizontally, a box is a stitch. Vertically, a box is a row. Charts are read from right to left on Right Side rows and from left to right on Wrong Side rows, as if the Right Side of the fabric were always facing you (even if you turn the piece around). Symbols for what stitch is being worked are included with the charts.

I cannot say enough about the importance of blocking. A garment isn't truly finished until it is blocked. It gives you the most accurate picture of what the dimensions are like and how the fabric will behave over the long haul. It smooths out stitches and "fudges" measurements. Pins are traditionally used to coax pieces to their proper size, but there are now blocking wires that scoot along the edges of the pieces to prevent pin "points." My preferred method is steaming with a light cloth over the garment. Another method is wet blocking, whereby the whole piece is wetted down and left to dry in the shape and size desired. Again, look to a good technique book for further information.

I cannot stress the importance of gauge enough, either. Swatching is essential to ensure that your stitches are the same size as those in our projects. This is crucial to getting the same measurements that the pattern calls for and making the garment fit. In some projects, gauge and measurements are not so important, but for garments, they are vital. Block the swatch and treat it as you would the garment. Ultimately you will launder your item and you will want to know sooner rather than later if the gauge will hold up. While you may be able to use blocking to compensate slightly for some size or shape problems, aim for accuracy in the first place. If you get more stitches per inch than called for, go up in needle size. If you get fewer stitches per inch than called for, go down in needle size. It is better to obtain the stitch gauge for width rather than the row gauge for length. Compensation for row gauge is easier to work out. Don't say you haven't been warned!

The Urban Knitter

Empire-Waisted, Sleeveless, A-Line, V-Neck Dress

| Stephanie Klose

CITY: Albany, NY

AGE: 24

Stephanie is a copyeditor for the New York State Bar Association and a terrific knitter. She lives in Albany's Center Square neighborhood, a district of restaurants, theaters, bars, shops, and quiet, tree-lined streets lined with rowhouses. She learned to knit when she was little but didn't do much with it until she got to college.

She was working on a philosophy degree and the tangible accomplishment knitting provided was a welcome foil to the esoteric class material. Taking weaving and spinning classes at a local arts center exposed her to ideas about color and texture and fabric structure, as well as expanding her resources for yarn sources and information. What she learned influenced her knitting both technically and artistically.

Stephanie knits for the pleasure of both the process and the product. As she puts it: "Knitting has enormous sensory appeal; the tactile pleasures of handling good fiber and the fabric it creates, the visual pleasures of color and texture. Knitting also has intellectual appeal; every pattern represents a theory for making a three-dimensional object out of a length of string. Knitters can delve as far as they like into the math behind it, or not at all, depending on the individual's inclination, and produce beautiful, functional objects either way." Stephanie has also begun to professionally design a few original patterns of her own.

Her taste in knitting runs to items that she can't find anywhere else: lace skirts, luxurious shawls, coats with tapestry-like colorwork, simple sweaters using gorgeous yarn, wild socks. She doesn't want to knit anything that looks like something she could have picked up at the mall. The dress she made for this project has the triple advantage of standing out in a crowd while having a universally flattering silhouette and being easy to knit. The microfiber ribbon used has beautiful sheen and drape.

Inspiration

From the start, Stephanie knew she wanted to knit a dress. She originally pictured a silhouette similar to the 1970s-era Diane von Furstenburg wrap dresses, but not a wrap: V-neck, elbow-length sleeves, nipped in at the waist, roughly knee-length, with a little swish around the hem. She had a number of good ideas we didn't put to use for this project, such as working in the round from the bottom up so newer knitters have all that fabric on which to gain confidence before having to deal with the neck or armholes. She thought the waist could be done with simple decreases all the way around instead of darts, and she liked the fit of raglan sleeves and knew they would be a lot less fussy than set-in sleeves.

Using her desire for a dress as a point of departure, I brought over a ready-to-wear dress from my closet to show her an empire waistline instead. I think many women find fitted waists not flattering to their figures. I personally like the way an empire waist covers the tummy area. I also thought of a sinfully slinky, drapey microfiber ribbon yarn.

Stephanie swatched and fell seriously in love with this yarn, deciding that it would make the sexiest, slinkiest dress imaginable. She also came up with the great idea of working the bottom skirt portion on the larger needles for drape and swish, imitating the look of a bias-cut skirt.

The ribbon is pretty heavy. Although loosening up the gauge would make it drape better (and work up faster), we needed stability at the shoulders where all the weight is supported. So I decided to work the bodice in a firmer gauge, from the bottom up, in pieces. For the skirt portion, stitches are picked up from the bottom of the bodice and worked from the top down, circularly, with increases for shaping. There are 6 increase points—each side "seam" and each "princess line" front and back, in roughly $1/4-1/2-1/4$ proportions. This mimics classic dressmaker lines.

Change to larger needles when the skirt gets about hip level. This way, you can stop at any point you feel the dress is long enough—or when you run out of yarn! We omitted the sleeves from

Stephanie's initial idea because of the weight of the yarn.

I took Stephanie's measurements and developed the schematics for her dress. It is a sleeveless, A-line, empire-waisted sheath with a V-neck. I planned a 35" bust with about 4" ease. Armholes are a somewhat shallow 7"; the front neck V is 6" deep. The empire line hits 14" from top of shoulder. Using her gauge, I plugged in the numbers and generated a pattern for her with the aid of my design software (I use both Garment Styler and Stitch Painter from Cochenille computer products).

I had Stephanie check out 51" for the skirt bottom by taking a tape measure and forming a circle of this length to see how it looked and moved. It is very important when working the skirt portion to hang up the work on a hanger for a while after finishing it, since the loosened gauge will grow the rows and shrink up width.

Stephanie loved the colorway of the hand-painted ribbon and thought the colors looked much better knitted up than they did in the skein. She liked the super-short color lengths. When knitted up, I think it's very reminiscent of a Monet watercolor.

Winding this yarn can be problematic. It needs to be wound into a ball by hand rather than using a winder. I put mine in an old pantyhose or a plastic baggie after winding it, to prevent tangling.

Although she had to figure out how to do the single-crochet edges, Stephanie thought these made a very tidy finish. It's a very good idea to bone up on some basic crochet skills as a supplement to knitting. Crocheted edges lend stability and support to such edges, and provide a nice, smooth look. Simple instructions are available in any book of general techniques.

Instructions | Empire-Waisted, Sleeveless, A-Line, V-Neck Dress

Slightly close-fitting

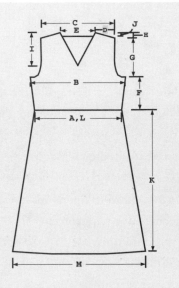

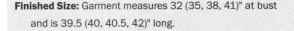

Finished Size: Garment measures 32 (35, 38, 41)" at bust and is 39.5 (40, 40.5, 42)" long.

Finished Measurements:

- **A.** Back/front bodice bottom = 14.5 (16, 17.75, 19)"
- **B.** Back/front bodice bust = 16 (17.5, 19, 20.5)"
- **C.** Across shoulder = 12 (13, 14, 15)"
- **D.** Each shoulder width = 3 (3.25, 3.5, 3.75)"
- **E.** Neck width = 6 (6.5, 7, 7.5)"
- **F.** Bodice length = 7"
- **G.** Armhole length = 6.5 (7, 7.5, 8)"
- **H.** Shoulder slope = 1"
- **I.** Front neck depth = 5.75 (6, 6.25, 6.75)"
- **J.** Back neck depth = 0.25"
- **K.** Skirt length = 26"
- **L.** Front/back skirt width at top = 14.5 (16, 17.5, 19)"

M. Front/back skirt width at bottom = 22.5 (24.25, 26.25, 27.75)"

Materials:

- Cherry Tree Hill Yarns "Glimmer" (100% nylon microfiber ribbon, 4oz, appx 247yds): 5 (6, 6, 7) skeins Dusk colorway.
- 24" circular knitting needles in sizes 6, 7, 8, 9, and 10, or whatever sizes it takes to get the gauges.
- Stitch markers.
- Crochet hook size E.

Gauge: 24 sts and 28 rows = 4" in Stockinette st on size 6 needles.

23 sts and 26 rows = 4" on size 7 needles.

22 sts = 4" on size 8 needles.

21 sts = 4" on size 9 needles.

20 sts = 4" on size 10 needles.

(Note: Make a swatch using all the needle sizes, then hang the swatch up to get a "hung" gauge, this gives the most accurate picture of the effects of gravity's pull on the sts.)

Special Notes: For the bodice, use the circular needles as if they were separate straight needles and work the pieces back and forth to produce flat pieces. For the skirt, join in a circle and work the rows around and around in a circular manner, with the Right Side, or outside, always facing you. You will then always knit to work Stockinette st.

Slip–slip–knit is described on page 25.

Back Bodice

Cast on with smallest needles 89 (97, 107, 115) sts. Work Stockinette st [p the Wrong Side rows and k the Right Side rows] and work until piece measures 1" total; end by finishing a Wrong Side row.

Shape for bust:

Next row or the Right Side [an Increase row]—k 2, increase 1 st, k to within the last 2 sts, increase 1 st, k the last 2 sts—91 (99, 109, 117) sts.

Work this Increase row on every 6th row 4 more times. Work even on 99 (107, 117, 125) sts until piece measures 6", end with a p row.

Shape armholes:

Bind off 6 (7, 8, 8) sts at the beginning of the next 2 rows—87 (93, 101, 109) sts remain. Bind off 2 (2, 2, 3) sts at the beginning of the next 2 rows—83 (89, 97, 103) sts remain.

Next row or the Right Side [a Decrease row]—k 2, k the next 2 sts together, k to last 4 sts, slip-slip knit the next 2 sts together, k last 2 sts—81 (87, 95, 101) sts remain.

Next row, or the Wrong Side—p across.

Repeat the last 2 rows 3 (3, 4, 4) times—there will be 2 less sts after each Right Side row worked. There are 75 (81, 87, 93) sts remaining after the last repeat.

Work 2 rows even, then repeat the Decrease row on next Right Side row—73 (79, 85, 91) sts.

Continue in Stockinette st until piece measures 12.5 (13, 13.5, 14)" total or 6.5 (7, 7.5, 8)" from the beginning of the armhole shaping, end with a p row.

Shape shoulders:

Bind off 4 (5, 5, 5) sts at the beginning of the next 2 rows—65 (69, 75, 81) sts remain. Bind off 4 (5, 5, 6) sts at the beginning of the next 2 rows—57 (59, 65, 69) sts remain. Bind off 5 (5, 6, 6) sts at the beginning of the next 2 rows and immediately after the last bind-off, work until there are 5 (5, 6, 6) sts on the right-hand needle, join another ball of yarn and bind off center 37 (39, 41, 45) sts, work to end, turn. With each shoulder's separate ball of yarn, bind off the remaining 5 (5, 6, 6) sts.

Front Bodice

Work exactly like the back bodice until the armholes measure 0.75 (1, 1.25, 1.25)", ending with a Wrong Side row.

Shape front neck:

Next row, a Right Side row—continue to finish shaping the armholes as you did for the back but bind off the single center st to begin the V-neck shaping.

Next row, a Wrong Side row—purl up to the bound-off center st, join another ball of yarn to the other side, and purl the other shoulder sts.

Continue to work both shoulders at the same time using their separate balls of yarn and on the Right Side rows, decrease at the V-neck as follows:

Left shoulder—k up to the last 3 sts from the neck edge, k the next 2 sts together as one, k the last st at edge. Right shoulder—with the other yarn at the beginning of the other neck edge, k 1, slip-slip-knit the next 2 sts together to decrease, k to the end.

Work this decrease on the Right Side rows another 17 (18, 19, 21) more times, then work even without decreasing. *At the same time,* when the armholes measure 6.5 (7, 7.5, 8)", shape the shoulders as you did for the back.

Steam the pieces to size and allow to dry. Sew the shoulders together, seam the sides together.

Skirt

With size 7 circular needles and Right Side facing you, pick up and k 1 st from each cast-on st along bottom edge of back—87 (95, 105, 113) sts, without seamed selvedge sts. Repeat for each st across front for 174 (190, 210, 226) sts total. Join beginning to end and place a stitch marker onto needle to mark this beginning/end of row and knitting circularly [in the round] with the Right Side facing you at all times, work in Stockinette [k all rows] for 1" total. Switch to size 8 circular needles and work for another 1". Switch to size 9 circular needles and work for another 1". Switch to size 10 circular needles and work for another 1".

Length of skirt, in inches	Number of stitches on needles
1.5	178 (194, 214, 230)
3.0	182 (198, 218, 234)
4.5	186 (202, 222, 238)
6.0	190 (206, 226, 242)
7.5	194 (210, 230, 246)
9.0	198 (214, 234, 250)
10.5	202 (218, 238, 254)
12.0	206 (222, 242, 258)
13.5	210 (226, 246, 262)
15.0	214 (230, 250, 266)
16.5	218 (234, 254, 270)
18.0	222 (238, 258, 274)
19.5	226 (242, 262, 278)

K next row as follows: ★k 22 (25, 28, 31), place marker of a second color to designate princess seam line (psl), k 43 (45, 49, 51), place another marker of second color for another psl, k 22 (25, 28, 31)★, place marker of a third color to designate side seam, repeat from ★ to ★. There are 4 psl markers, a side-seam marker, and a beginning/end of row marker altogether.

† First Increase row—k and ‡ increase before next psl marker, then after next psl marker ‡, work past side-seam marker, repeat from ‡ to ‡, work to end—178 (194, 214, 230) sts.

Work even for another 1.5".

Next Increase row—k 1, increase, k to within 1 st of side-seam marker, increase, k to 1 st of after side-seam marker, increase, k to within 1 st of end, increase, k last st—182 (198, 218, 234) sts.

Work for another 1.5".†

Repeat from † to † having 4 more sts with each Increase row. See box on page 6 to help keep track.

When skirt measures 20", there are 226 (242, 262, 278) sts. Work [a round of purl, then a round of knit] 2 times, work a round of purl, then bind off very loosely in knit.

Finishing

Block skirt to measurements.

With Right Side facing you, trim borders by working a row of single-crochet evenly around each armhole edge and around neck edge.

◇ Log Cabin Baby Blanket | Michelle Fiander

CITY: Indianapolis, IN
AGE: 36

Steven J. Schmidt

Michelle is a librarian, with a master's in library science and another in English. Prior to this, she was an editor, teaching assistant, bartender, and waitress. She's originally from Halifax, Nova Scotia, Canada, but has been living in Indianapolis for almost three years.

She learned how to knit and purl from her mother when she was young. Michelle knit her first sweater, a Lopi, when she was in high school. During her twenties she knit two sweaters (both cardigans) but didn't become really fascinated by knitting until five years ago. She was living in a very small town and had a lot of time on her hands.

Thus, with the help of an expert knitter friend,

Ruthmary, Michelle began work on an Aran sweater. She had always wanted to do cables and such, but she thought the design would be really difficult. However, once she got the hang of it, she was surprised at how easy it was, although even now she phones her friend for long-distance help when she hits a snag on a project. Having a mentor to help you through the confusing bits is pretty important!

Michelle says she's not always the most patient person in the world, but for some reason she has a lot of patience with knitting. She's ripped projects back and started from scratch a number of times, but hasn't felt frustrated by this in the least. Knitting is the closest she comes to Zen! Her knitting style is a bit awkward. She moves her entire hand to carry the yarn and doesn't think she's as fast as many knitters. She says, "Maybe sometime I'll be able to relearn how to hold and move the yarn. Until then, I'll keep on going as I have been."

This baby blanket is very easy, a good project for a beginner. The directional design makes an interesting change from straight Garter stitch. Having completed this, Michelle says she is now looking forward to trying some of the other designs in this book.

Inspiration

Both Michelle and I have been knitting a lot of baby blankets lately. I laughingly surmise that our friends are in the procreating stages of their lives. Michelle was therefore more than amenable to working one out for the book.

The variegated bulky yarn is soft enough for little ones. More importantly, it's washable. This is a tantamount concern when designing for children. What struck me most, however, was the fabulous coloration of this yarn. Unlike most variegated yarns on the market, our nicely textured "krinkle-spun" mock-bouclé comes with *long* stretches of the same color. That is, the changes of color occur infrequently. In terms of design, this means chunks of color rather than short stripes when knit.

To take full advantage of this unique character-istic, I planned a "log cabin" type of construction. As in quilting, begin with a patch in the middle. Short and wide patches are knitted onto each side edge after rotating the whole piece successively. The effect is truly stunning. Literally, this blanket will turn heads. It seems like many yarn changes occurred, when in fact only one yarn was used.

As with many of the other projects, the real beauty of this piece is that it looks far more difficult than it is. Michelle really enjoyed making this piece. The trick to having the work appear even is to bind off *loosely* with each strip or patch. Try a larger needle size just for this bind-off alone.

Michelle confessed to having had slight problems with picking up stitches along completed edges. She found it difficult to identify which part of the loop to pick up from. What you are looking for is a "chain." The needle should go under both the loops that form the chain. I suggest using a crochet hook to aid in this. After picking up a stitch with the hook, be sure to place it on the needle with the twist consistent with your knitting. In other words, see how your stitches normally lie on the needle. Any new, added-on stitches should lie in the same direction.

Although it's ideal for beginners, the structure of this piece makes Garter stitch so palatable that even seasoned knitters will find it interesting and intriguing to do. The bulky yarn also ensures quick progress.

Instructions | Log Cabin Baby Blanket

Worked by rotating and picking up around a rectangle

Finished Size: about 35" × 40"

Materials:

- Lion Brand "Homespun" (98% acrylic, 2% polyester, 6oz/170g, appx 185yds/169m): 4 skeins color #315 Tudor.
- Size 10.5 knitting needles, or whatever size it takes to get the gauge.

Gauge: 12 sts and 24 rows = 4" in Garter st (k every row).

Special Notes: Each section of this log cabin construction is worked by rotating piece and picking up sts along previous sections. Be sure to bind off each section loosely.

Begin with Garter st rectangle in the center. Cast on 9 sts and work in Garter for about 4" but *slip* the first st knitwise at the beginning of each row to form a chain at the side edges (this will make it easy to pick up side edges later). Bind off *loosely*, leaving last loop on needle. Mark this side as Right Side (RS).

Rotate the rectangle 90° clockwise (with RS facing you) and pick up 1 st in each chain along former left edge (2 rows = 1 ridge; there are as many sts as there are Garter ridges). Work in Garter st for 2" and don't forget to slip the first sts for chained edge. End by binding off on a RS row (that's the same side that faced you when you picked up the sts), leaving last loop on needle.

Rotate the rectangle 90° clockwise and pick up 1 st in each chain along former left edge of your 2" (there are as many sts as there are Garter ridges) *as well as* 1 st in each st of bottom cast-on edge. Work Garter for another 2" and don't forget to slip the first sts for chained edge. End by binding off on a RS row (that's the same side that faced you when you picked up the sts).

Rotate the rectangle 90° clockwise and pick up 1 st in each chain along former left edge of your 2" (there are as many sts as there are Garter ridges) *as well as* 1 st in each chain of *other* side edge of original center rectangle. Work Garter for another 2" and don't forget to slip the first sts for chained edge. End by binding off on a RS row (that's the same side that faced you when you picked up the sts).

Rotate the rectangle 90° clockwise and pick up 1 st in each chain along former left edge of your 2" (there are as many sts as there are Garter ridges) *as well as* 1 st in each st of the top bound-off edge sts of original center rectangle *and* 1 st in each chain along other side edge 2". Work Garter for another 2" and don't forget to slip the first sts for chained edge. End by binding off on a RS row (that's the same side that faced you when you picked up the sts).

Continue to rotate and pick up; this is a log cabin style, like in quilting. When piece measures approximately 35" wide by 40" long, complete last rectangle and fasten off last loop.

Since the yarn shades gradually, this will form an intriguing and intricate-looking pattern with very little effort!

Finishing

Block piece to smooth and even out.

🌀 Apron-Front Halter Top | Jessica M.T.F. Thomas

Lily M. Chin

CITY: Boston, MA
AGE: 29

Jessica was born in San Francisco but raised in Wisconsin. Her mom indoctrinated her with fiber-love by curating and repairing oriental rugs as a home-based business. Her dad, now retired, is an avid art lover and fisherman with an appreciation for all handwork.

Jessica received her BFA from the University of Wisconsin at Madison in 1999. She currently lives in Boston and was married in 2000. She expects to receive a Master of Fine Arts in studio art from the School of the Museum of Fine Arts, Boston, in affiliation with Tufts University by May 2002.

In her studio art work, she visually pursues notions of the subjective approach to universal, discoverable "truths" through a language of geometric abstraction and fractal, interlocking design motifs. Her ideas get worked out in egg tempera and oil paints, digital printing, lithographic and screen printing, animation, sound, and film work. She also works sculpturally, exploring both the loss of public, ritual, and emotional activity in our culture as well as the comfortable mental cages we build for ourselves in order to function in our everyday lives.

The interlocking stitches of knitting make it perfect for her sculptural work, as does its obsessive, repetitive nature. Although Jessica works in two, three, and four dimensions, the pattern of repetitive production runs through all her work, as do motifs of interlocking hexagonal lattices, and scrims or veils of dots or pixels as the marks that present the image to the viewer.

In her "domestic" knitting, she loves simply being able to fit garments to her figure, a "zaftig" six feet two. Since her figure often demands resizing standard patterns, she started learning design principles a few years ago. Pretty soon the fiber junkie in her was sponging up knowledge of yarn behavior (and misbehavior) and how different fabrics behave, and learning to design for herself.

She also still knits from patterns and does a lot of Stockinette or Seed stitch on size 2 to 4 needles while commuting on the train, mainly for stress relief and to exercise (exorcize?) that Puritan work ethic she was raised on. Since her artwork is emotionally demanding, she says "it's great to kick back and make something without having to think about what it means!"

Inspiration

Jessica chose the halter top as a design challenge for both of us, since there really aren't any good, modest halter patterns out there. Two-strap tank tops are found in every summer issue of every major knitting magazine. The halter is a fresh, fun garment for summer, especially in the color palette this tape-yarn offers. This yarn is unusual among tapes in that there's actually some stretch to it! The texture is also most alluring.

Jessica's tastes run toward vintage (1940s), so the apron-front styling and muted celery color suited her. It is updated by the yarn, however. Jessica's concerns were with bust support, fabric buckles at the neck, and a sagging lower back. She also wanted to do minimal sewing.

By keeping the back high with enough coverage at the sides and neck, I designed the halter to accommodate either a strapless or a halter-type bra. This took care of the support issue. I then thought about stitch and construction until solutions fell into place. Each stitch pattern has its own intrinsic characteristics. Garter rows are far shorter than Stockinette rows. Since the piece is worked from side to side rather than from the bottom up, Garter acts as a rib at the edges. This pulls in slightly for all the trims, especially at the neck, sides, and back. It also pulls in at the waist for a fitted shape, while Stockinette is full for the bust (again, that's a function of the differences in row gauge). Garter on its side also has enough lateral spread to prevent droopy back!

It was a really novel construction to Jessica, but made complete sense. As for the actual knitting up, she found that her wooden needles stuck to the yarn so much it really dragged and just about shredded the yarn. She recommends metal or bamboo needles (i.e., something smooth) for this project. She also found that, if you rip it out, the yarn gets wrinkled up when reknitted. A light touch of a *cool* iron may smooth it back out. It's nylon, so place a handkerchief over the yarn first (unless you *like* sticky irons).

Jessica says: Add a shrug, shawl, or cardigan and you get an instant twinset! Use furry yarn for the edges (using intarsia) and pair it with a formal skirt for evening wear, especially wonderful with opera-length gloves (also hand knit, of course).

Instructions | Apron-Front Halter Top
Shaped and close-fitting

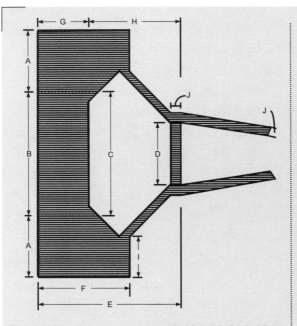

Finished Size: Garment measures 17 (18.5, 20, 21.5, 23)" at front bust, 22 (24, 26, 28, 30)" all around waist, and is 12 (14, 15, 16, 17)" long.

Finished Measurements:
- A. Half back waist = 5.5 (6, 6.5, 7, 7.5)"
- B. Full front waist = 11 (12, 13, 14, 15)"
- C. Front bust = 17 (18.5, 20, 21.5, 23)"
- D. Neck width = 6"
- E. Body length = 13 (14, 15, 16, 17)"

- F. Back waist height= 9"
- G. Front waist height = 5"
- H. Front bodice height with neck border = 8 (9, 10, 11, 12)"
- I. Top of back straight edge = 4"
- J. Neck border and straps = 1"

Materials:
- Trendsetter "Balboa" (36% cotton, 36% acrylic, 28% polyamide, 50g, appx 150yds): 3 (4, 4, 4, 4) skeins #20 Celery.
- Size 9 knitting needles, or whatever size it takes to get the gauge.
- Stitch markers.

Gauge:
  20 sts and 26 rows= 4" in Stockinette st [k on Right
    Side rows, p on Wrong Side rows].
  20 sts and 40 rows= 4" in Garter st [k all rows].

Special Notes: The whole piece is worked from side to side beginning at center of back, working from left back to left front to right front to right back and seamed at the center back. Stitch markers help distinguish Garter st borders (which eventually become the straps) from rest of knitting. Slip st markers as you work.

Beginning at the center back, you will cast on for the *length* of the back, which is fairly high up, and work in Garter stitch for stretch in this vertical direction. This will also hold up better, with no flopping down.

Then you'll begin some Stockinette in a *gradual* substitution or replacement of Garter at the bust end, yet keep about 5 sts at the very top for border-into-strap. This works fabulously since Stockinette is a bit longer than Garter and fills out just-so to accommodate some bust. You'll also begin to increase at the top edge, all the while maintaining 5 sts in Garter at top for border. Ultimately, the Garter at bottom (waist) end will taper off at a couple of inches from the bottom of the bust.

When increases are completed and straps are to begin, do *only* the 5 sts of Garter border for length of strap/back tie (I actually decreased it down to 3 sts halfway for less bulk). After completing strap, break off yarn. Rejoin, with Right Side facing you, along the *side edge* of strap about 10 rows away from remaining body stitches. Pick up and knit 5 sts from this side edge to regain the border; work remainder of row to reconnect. Work straight for top "apron" neck of halter until ready for other strap, then break off yarn.

Work other strap next. Substitute 5 strap stitches in lieu of 5 border stitches at top of halter neck by knitting end stitch of strap *together* with each con-secutive stitch of border every 2 rows. When 5 strap stitches become the border stitches again, reverse everything.

Decrease at neck edge, and gradually reduce the Stockinette portion of the bust. Sew last row to the cast-on edge to finish.

Center and Left Back

Cast on 47 sts.

Row 1 [mark this side as Right Side (RS)]—slip the first st as if to p with the yarn in front to form a smooth chained selvedge, bring the yarn to the back between the needles in order to k, then k across.

All rows—repeat Row 1 until 40 rows have been completed or until work measures 4", ending ready to work a Right Side, or odd-numbered, row.

Begin shaping for armholes and begin Stockinette st for bust:

Next row—slip the first st as before, k the next 4 sts for 5 sts worked total, place a st marker onto needle to differentiate border, work increase, place another st marker onto needle, k to end—48 sts with 1 [increased] st between the st markers.

Next row [Wrong Side]—continue to work Garter st *but* work Stockinette st on the one st between the st markers.

Next row—slip the first st as before, k the next 4 sts for 5 sts worked total, slip marker, increase in next st, k the st itself, remove marker, k the next st, place marker back onto needle, k to end—49 sts with 3 sts between the st markers.

Next row and *all Wrong Side rows*—continue to work Garter st *but* work Stockinette st over the sts between the st markers.

Next row—slip the first st as before, k the next 4 sts for 5 sts worked total, slip marker, increase in next st, k to marker, remove marker, k the next st, place marker back onto needle, k to end—50 sts with 2 more sts between the st markers than before.

Repeat last 2 rows with an extra st total after every 2 rows and an extra 2 sts of Stockinette st between the markers. Work until there are a total of 33 sts between the markers and 26 sts of Garter at the left side of marker on a Right Side row.

Keep this bottom edge constant at 26 Garter sts but continue to increase at the beginning of the Right Side rows after the first 5 Garter sts. Work until there are 67 (72, 77, 82, 87) sts total, ending with a Wrong Side row.

Form one strap:

Next row on the Right Side—work *only* the first 5 sts in Garter st, slipping the first st as before; do *not* work the other remaining sts. Continue to work these 5 sts in this manner.

When the strap over these 5 sts measures 8", slip first st, slip next st as if to knit, k next 2 sts together, then pass the closest slipped st over this decreased st, k last st—3 sts.

Work Garter st over these 3 sts for another 12", slipping the first st as before. Slip the first st as if to knit, k next 2 sts together, then pass the slipped st over this decreased st—1 st remains. Fasten off and end off yarn.

Continue front:

With the Right Side facing you, join yarn to 5th chain at side edge of strap just completed closest to body. Pick up and k 1 st for each of the 5 chains, place marker, and keep these 5 sts in Garter st. Continue in established Stockinette and Garter. Work on 67 (72, 77, 82, 87) sts again until Garter st neck edge measures 6" from picked-up row, ending with a Wrong Side row. Break off yarn and keep sts on needle.

Form other strap:

Make a slipknot on needle, [knit, purl, and knit] all in the same slipknot—3 sts. Work Garter st over these 3 sts for 12", slipping first st as before.

Next row—work first st, in next st (the center st) work [knit, purl, and knit] all in the same st, k last st. Work Garter st as before over these 5 sts for another 8". If working strap on same needle as body sts, end with strap sts on same needle as body.

Join strap to body:

With Right Side of body facing you, k 4 strap sts, k next st of strap *together* with first st of neck border, turn, sl first st, k 4. ★ k 4 strap sts, k next st of strap *together* with next st of border, turn, sl first st, k 4; repeat from ★ 3 more times.

The 5 strap sts have now substituted for the 5 Garter st border sts and there are still 67 (72, 77, 82, 87) sts. Work 2 rows in established patterns.

Shape for other side of body:

Keeping to patterns, all shapings will now be reversed.

Next row—work 5 Garter st border sts, k 2 together to decrease in the Stockinette portion, work to end in established patterns—66 (71, 76, 81, 86) sts. Continue to decrease at the beginning of the Right Side rows after the first 5 Garter sts

in this same manner. There is 1 less st after every 2 rows. Work until there are 64 sts total and 33 Stockinette sts between the markers; end with a Wrong Side row.

Next row—work 5 Garter st border sts, continue to decrease next 2 Stockinette sts together, k to within 1 st of next marker, place new marker onto needle, k 1, remove next marker, k to end—27 Garter sts at bottom edge with 31 Stockinette sts between the st markers. Work a Wrong Side row.

Repeat last 2 rows with one less st total after every 2 rows and 2 less sts of Stockinette st between the markers and 1 more Garter st at bottom edge. Work until there are a total of 47 sts and no more Stockinette sts between the markers.

Work in Garter st on these 47 sts for another 4", bind off.

Finishing

Block pieces to measurements. Sew back seam by sewing cast-on edge to bound-off edge.

Ribbed Scarf, Hat, and Mittens
Daniel Pepper Herrera
CITY: Seattle, WA
AGE: 31

Lily M. Chin

Daniel was born in Tuscon, Arizona. When he was five, his aunt Mary (who is just nine years older than him) tried to teach herself to knit to alleviate what would now be considered ADD or Attention Deficit Disorder. She didn't take to it very well. The piece she had started got tucked away in Daniel's grandmother's cupboard.

Daniel, being a nosy kid, found it a couple of years later. He also found some old *Better Homes & Gardens* magazines of his grandmother's (the kind with "how-to's") and took to knitting as a challenge and a puzzle. Nobody really thought much about it, as he was a quiet child and enter-

tained himself a lot. Little did they know that at age nine, Daniel was riding his bicycle to the local yarn shop and getting more ideas for things he wanted to create.

A lot of men complain about being the only guy in a group of knitters or getting unusual stares, but try being a nine-year-old boy in a yarn store without a parent around! Ha! You should have seen the look on some of the shop owners' faces. Yet they started to educate Daniel and pointed him in the right directions. It was wonderful for him! He's never looked back since. Tatting and crochet and all the various forms of needlework are nice in their own way, but one long piece of string and a couple of pointed sticks feel much more harmonious to Daniel.

Fast-forward fifteen years: Even during the six years he was in the navy as a computer tech, Daniel was knitting in his off time. It became a form of meditation and a connection to his roots when he was so far away from home. Again, he received comments and questions. Yet when they began to realize the time and effort involved in making something by hand, his fellow officers gained a whole new appreciation for the sweaters they themselves were receiving from home. Some even wanted to learn, and started making things for their own wives and children.

Daniel now lives in a great city full of art and of people looking for something new to do. He's not sure what it is that attracts people to knitting, but he thinks they want to be able to create something themselves. Daniel states: "In the busy world we live in, it's a way of taking 'me' time, of preserving a small snapshot of who and where we are. I've taught a lot of my friends, both men and women, to knit. We have a lot of fun when we can all get together and spend a little time to create over a good mocha while listening to some jazz at the local coffeehouse."

Inspiration

Although Daniel's friends and family consider him a nonconformist, he's also a traditionalist. He likes things that are versatile and classic. Simple, clean lines are the key to who he is. He wanted something easy and quick with universal appeal. I originally thought these would be great "guy" accessories. However, I see no reason why anyone can't wear them.

They are quite versatile and adaptable. The mittens are interchangeable, fitting either hand, and the hat and scarf can be made longer or shorter depending on your taste and comfort level. Daniel prefers shorter hats himself so his ears can hear everything around him. If, however, your ears get colder than his, add a couple of inches to cuff it and it'll still look great.

Be sure to work tight, firm bind-offs so that the ribs do not flair out. If need be, go down a needle size or two in order to accomplish this. The knitting is so basic, some call it mindless. Others refer to it as TV knitting. It's a perfect concomitant to other activities. I've known people to knit at their computers while waiting for long downloads. I think of this type of knitting as "potential multitasking."

A blend of superfine alpaca and wool, the yarn makes these accessories extra cozy. The charcoal will go with just about anything in anyone's wardrobe. Since knitters often give the fruits of their labor away as loving gifts, we've sized these for both children and adults. Make a few sizes in several colors for last-minute or emergency situations.

Ribbed Hat, Scarf, and Mittens

Materials:

- Cascade "Lana D'Oro" (50% superfine alpaca, 50% wool, 50g/1.75oz, appx 110yds) #223 Charcoal Gray Heather: 7 skeins for the whole Adult set.

Instructions | Ribbed Ascot Scarf

Shown in Adult version

Finished Size: Average Child (Adult)

Finished Measurements: 5 (8)" × 44 (44)"

Materials:

- 2 (3) skeins.
- Size 7 knitting needles, or whatever size it takes to get the gauge.

Gauge: 24 sts and 26 rows = 4" in 2 × 2 Ribbing when slightly stretched after steam blocking.

Cast on 34 (58) sts.

Row 1—slip first st as if to k with yarn in back, k 1, [p 2, k 2] across.

Row 2—slip first st as if to p with yarn in front, p 1, [k 2, p 2] across.

Repeat Rows 1 and 2 until work measures about 44"; bind off very tightly in Ribbing.

Steam block lightly to soften and to bring out Ribbing.

Instructions | Ribbed Watch Cap
Shown in Adult cuffed version

Finished Size: Average Child (Adult)

Finished Measurements: Lower edge circumference = about 20 (22)" around.

Materials:
- 1 (3) skeins. (Note: This is for uncuffed Child and for cuffed Adult. Add an extra skein to Child for cuffed; subtract a skein for Adult uncuffed.)
- 16" circular knitting needles in size 7 or whatever size it takes to get the gauge, and a spare needle of same size or smaller for binding off.
- Stitch marker.

Gauge: 24 sts and 26 rows = 4" in 2 × 2 Ribbing when slightly stretched after steam blocking.

Cast on 120 (132) sts with 16" circular needles. Place a st marker onto the needle to signify the beginning and end of the rounds, slipping marker as you work. Join beginning to end, being careful not to twist the work. Work 2 × 2 Ribbing st as follows:

All rows—[k 2, p 2] around; Right Side faces you at all times.

Work until piece measures 4.5 (11.5)" [This length is up to the individual. If you want a cuff for the Child, make it a couple of inches more; if you do not want a cuff for the Adult, end off at perhaps 6.5" or so].

Next row—[k 2, p 2 tog] around—90 (99) sts.

Continue in k 2, p 1 Ribbing for another 2" or so.

Bind-off:
Turn hat inside out and place needles side by side with points facing same direction.

With spare needle, ★ knit one stitch from each needle together and bind off as it is finished [also known as 3-needle bind-off].

Repeat from ★ across row. For larger size, k last st and bind it off. Fasten off at the end. Break yarn, leaving an 8" tail.

Tuck:

Thread yarn on a blunt sewing needle and pull it through to the Right Side by going through the corner that was just made. Turn hat Right Side out.

Bring the corners together on the Right Side and stitch them together a minimum of 4 times, then stitch them down to the center of the seam that runs along the top. Turn hat inside out and weave in all loose ends.

Steam block lightly to soften and to bring out Ribbing.

Instructions | Ribbed Mittens

Shown in Child version

Finished Size: Average Child (Small Adult, Large Adult)

Finished Measurements:
- A. Cuff circumference = about 4.5 (6.5, 8)" around.
- B. Hand circumference = about 6.5 (8.5, 10.5)" around.
- C. Height = variable, but ours were 8 (9, 10)" from tip to bottom.

Materials:
- 1 (2, 2) skeins.
- Size 7 knitting needles, or whatever size it takes to get the gauge, and a spare knitting needle of same size or smaller for binding off.

Gauge:
24 sts and 26 rows = 4" in 2 × 2 Ribbing when slightly stretched after steam blocking.
20 sts and 26 rows = 4" in Stockinette st [k on Right Side, p on Wrong Side].

Special Note: Slip-slip-knit = [slip next st as if to knit] twice, insert the left-hand needle from left to right through the fronts of these 2 sts, then knit the two together in this position [through their back loops].

Cast on 30 (42, 50) sts.

Row 1 [Right Side]—k 2, [p 2, k 2] across.

Row 2 [Wrong Side]—p 2, [k 2, p 2] across.

Repeat Rows 1 and 2 until work measures about 2.5 (3, 3)", ending with a Wrong Side row.

Next row [Right Side]—k across and increase 2 stitches evenly spaced—32 (44, 52) sts.

Next row [Wrong Side]—p across.

Next row—k across.

Work 3 rows in Stockinette or to bottom of where the thumb begins, end ready to work a Right Side row.

Begin thumb gusset:

Row 1—k 15 (21, 25), increase, k 2, increase, k 15 (21, 25)—34 (46, 54) sts.

Row 2 and *all even or Wrong Side rows*—p across.

Row 3—k 15 (21, 25), increase, k 4, increase, k 15 (21, 25)—36 (48, 56) sts.

Row 5—k 15 (21, 25), increase, k 6, increase, k 15 (21, 25)—38 (50, 58) sts.

Row 7—k 15 (21, 25), increase, k 8, increase, k 15 (21, 25)—40 (52, 60) sts.

Row 9—k 15 (21, 25), increase, k 10, increase, k 15 (21, 25)—42 (54, 62) sts.

For Child size, stop here.

Row 11—k 0 (21, 25), increase, k 12, increase, k 0 (21, 25)—0 (56, 64) sts.

Row 13—k 0 (21, 25), increase, k 14, increase, k 0 (21, 25)—0 (58, 66) sts.

For Small Adult size, stop here.

Row 15—k 0 (0, 25), increase, k 16, increase, k 0 (0, 25)—0 (0, 68) sts.

Row 17—k 0 (0, 25), increase, k 18, increase, k 0 (0, 25)—0 (0, 70) sts.

Begin thumb:

Row 1 [Wrong Side]—p 27 (37, 45), bring yarn to the back, slip next st, bring yarn to the front, place slipped st back onto left-hand needle to complete a wrap, turn.

Row 2 [Right Side]—k 12 (16, 20), turn.

Row 3—p 12 (16, 20), turn.

Repeat last 2 rows 1 (3, 5) more times.

First decrease row [Right Side]—k 1, ★slip-slip-knit [ssk] to decrease, k 1 (3, 5), k 2 together [k2tog] to decrease; repeat from ★ once, k 1, turn—8 (12, 16) sts.

Next row—p 8 (12, 16), turn.

For Child size, stop here.

Second decrease row—k 1, ★ssk to decrease, k 0 (1, 3), k2tog to decrease; repeat from ★ once, k 1, turn—0 (8, 12) sts.

Next row—p 0 (8, 12), turn.

For Small Adult size, stop here.

Third decrease row—k 1, ★ssk to decrease, k 0 (0, 1), k2tog to decrease; repeat from ★ once, k 1, turn—0 (0, 8) sts.

Next row—p 0 (0, 8), turn.

For all sizes:

Next row [Right Side]—k 1, slip 1 as if to k, k2tog, pass the slipped st over this decrease, k 3 together to decrease, k 1, turn—4 sts remain.

Next row—bind off all 4 stitches, break yarn, leaving a 7" tail to sew thumb seam later.

Body of hand:

Join yarn with Wrong Side facing you and p remaining 15 (21, 25) sts on left-hand needle from Row 10 (14, 18) before beginning of thumb.

Row 11 (15, 19)—k 30 (42, 50).

Row 12 (16, 20)—p 30 (42, 50).

Continue in Stockinette or repeat last 2 rows 5 (6, 7) more times or until piece reaches the little finger; end ready to work a Right Side row.

Fingertips:

First decrease row—k 1, ★ssk to decrease, k 10 (16, 20), k2tog to decrease; repeat from ★ once, k 1—26 (38, 46) sts.

Next row—p across.

Second decrease row—k 1, ★ssk to decrease, k 8 (14, 18), k2tog to decrease; repeat from ★ once, k 1—22 (34, 42) sts.

Next row—p across.

Third decrease row [Right Side]—k 1, ★ssk to decrease, k 6 (12, 16), k2tog to decrease; repeat from ★ once, k 1—18 (30, 38) sts.

Fourth decrease row [Wrong Side]—p 1, ★p 2 together [p2tog] to decrease, p 4 (10, 14), slip

each of next 2 sts individually as if to knit, place them back onto left-hand needle as if to p, p these 2 sts together through their *back* loops; repeat from ★ once, p 1—14 (26, 34) sts.

For Child size, stop here.

Fifth decrease row—k 1, ★ssk, k 0 (8, 12), k2tog; repeat from ★ once, k 1—0 (22, 30) sts.

Sixth decrease row—p 1, ★p2tog, p 0 (6, 10), p2tog through their back loops; repeat from ★ once, p 1—0 (18, 26) sts.

For all sizes:

Seventh decrease row—k 1, ssk, k 2 (4, 8), k2tog—12 (16, 24) sts.

Lay needles parallel to each other with Right Sides facing together and Wrong Sides to the outside, having 5 (7, 11) sts toward you and 7 (9, 13) sts away from you. With spare needle, knit first st from each needle together. Next, ★knit 1 st from the front needle with 2 sts from the back needle together (3 sts together total)★. There are now 2 sts on the right-hand needle. Pass first stitch over the second for first bind-off.

Now knit 1 st from each needle together and bind off the same way until there are 2 sts on the front needle and 3 sts on the back needle.

Repeat from ★ to ★ and bind off, then bind off the last sts from each needle together.

Fasten off and break yarn, leaving an 8" tail.

Seam sides and thumbs, weave in loose ends. Steam block if desired.

Easy, Reversible, Two-Toned Scarf (or Stole)

| Sarah Farley

Mark Peiker

CITY: Denver, CO

AGE: 30

Sarah grew up in Denver, but went to Michigan State University where she studied business/hotel restaurant management. After college she moved to Minneapolis and went to work in human resources in the hospitality industry, but after six years of hotels she decided to take her H.R. knowledge to other industries. She frankly needed to get out of twenty-four-hour operations and make a little more money! She moved back to Denver six years ago and is now a recruiter, finding the best candidates to fill job openings.

Sarah began knitting when she was sixteen, on a vacation in Lincoln, Nebraska, visiting her extended family. Nearly everyone in her family knits—and let's face it, there's not a lot for a sixteen-year-old to do in Lincoln. In order to fight boredom, her mom taught her how to knit. (It should be mentioned that Mom is noted knitwear designer Sidna Farley.)

The first thing Sarah made was a bulky, vertically striped sweater without a pattern (it helps when you have a knitting instructor as a mother). She's made many sweaters, socks, hats, gloves, scarves, and baby clothes, but Sarah is not one of those knitters who always has a project going or has multiple projects going at any given time.

She finds it humorous when people find out that she knits because she always gets the reaction *You knit?* or *You* made *that?*

Inspiration

When I first invited Sarah to join our project, she loved the idea. However, she thought the timing bad: Her work schedule was on overload, she was traveling quite a lot, and she was in the middle of a job change.

I really wanted her included and swore up and down that all she had to do was a scarf. I promised to do everything but the knitting for her. Happily, she relented.

To create a scarf that wouldn't bore Sarah to tears yet would be simple enough to handle during a time of high stress was a challenge. I've always had my own notions for scarves. It has to be reversible. It has to feel fabulous around the neck. It has to drape well.

I wanted colorwork of some kind. But the backside of intarsia or Fair Isle or even mosaic slip-stitching is always messy and ungainly. I then thought of stripes in a knit-purl combination. The change of color in knits will be smooth but in purls, colors blend or bleed (see Greg's project, page 94). Alternate the two stitches and front and back will be the same! This is nothing but fancier two-row stripes.

I chose yarns that were irresistible: a soft cotton chenille against a subtly hairy and tweedy angora. The two worked well together, providing high texture with enough contrast between them. The colors also contrasted well yet were harmonious. Sarah loved working with them. The combination of yarns, stitch, and slightly loose gauge made for a wonderfully drapey fabric.

A stole is nothing but an enlarged scarf, so I've included directions for this as well. The scarf looked and felt too good not to wrap around the whole body. I can't wait to coddle myself in my own version later.

☼ **Instructions** | Easy, Reversible, Two-Toned Scarf (or Stole)

Finished Size: About 9" wide and 72" long. For a stole, about 18" × 72".

Materials:

- For color A: Aurora/Garnstudio "Cotton Frisé" (85% cotton, 15% polyamid, 50g, appx 109 yds): 2 skeins #9 Lime (4 skeins for the stole)
- For color B: Aurora/Garnstudio "Karisma Angora-Tweed" (30% angora, 70% wool, 50g, appx 113 yds): 2 skeins #03 Medium Slate Blue (4 skeins for the stole)
- Size 6 knitting needles, or whatever size it takes to get the gauge.

Gauge: 18 sts = 4" in Pattern st (a multiple of 6 sts plus 5 extra).

Special Note: Do not cut the yarns but leave at side edge, carrying them up loosely until ready to pick up and work with again.

With color A, cast on 41 sts (83 sts for a stole).
Work Pattern st as follows:

Row 1—change to color B, slip the first st as if you're going to knit it off from left needle onto right needle, ★k 3 and p 3; repeat from ★ across, then end with k 3 and p 1.

Row 2—with color B, repeat Row 1.

Row 3—change to color A and repeat Row 1.

Row 4—with color A, repeat Row 1.

Repeat Rows 1 through 4 until work measures 72" or desired length, end by finishing with Row 1 of the Pattern st.

End color B, bind off in Pattern st with color A, end off.

⟨⟩ Lace Capelet | Buffie Hollis

CITY: New Orleans, LA
AGE: 33

F. Tobias Morris

An archivist in New Orleans, Buffie has lived in the Big Easy for three years now and she says it's great! She lives in an old apartment building on St. Charles Avenue, not in the Garden District, but directly outside it in the Uptown neighborhood. She's actually on the Mardi Gras parade route for the Uptown parades like Bacchus, Orpheus, and Rex. It can get a little hairy at times, especially since she's not really a party person. But interesting things do happen. A neighbor had a band playing in her courtyard (which is *small*) before Bacchus 2000. They weren't too bad, luckily, since she couldn't get away from them without leaving her apartment.

Buffie grew up in Kansas, and after getting a B.A. in history she decided to specialize in public history. She went to graduate school at the University of California in Riverside, where she earned a master's in history with a specialty in historic preservation. Then she moved to Pennsylvania. While there, she decided she really wanted to become an archivist and enrolled in the School of Information Sciences at the University of Pittsburgh. After leaving there with another master's degree, this time in library and information sciences with a concentration in archival management, she got a job with the New Orleans Notarial Archives.

The New Orleans Archives have a collection of notarial acts from 1763 to the present. It's a pretty fascinating place to work. She takes the streetcar to and from work, so there's plenty of time to knit!

"It feels like I've been knitting all my life," Buffie says, "but really it's only been since age ten or twelve. My mom has always crocheted and I remember watching her when I was young. But I was fascinated by her collection of knitting needles and would play with them. It was actually my grandmother, though, who taught me to knit. She taught me basic knit and purl and then I just started following patterns on my own. It's only been in the last five years or so that I've developed a really serious interest in it. I discovered Kathy's Kreations in Ligonier, Pennsylvania, while I was preparing to return to graduate school. Kathy Zimmerman, the shop owner, is a great lady and was always very helpful and encouraging. We do have a couple of adequate yarn shops here, though."

Buffie likes to knit more complicated designs, and hates knitting more than one of the same thing. She's also really into fine-gauge things.

Inspiration

A shawl is a project Buffie had been thinking of for a while. Yet she hadn't been able to find a good pattern that she liked. She wants to do one that would keep her shoulders warm while reading in the winter (yes, it does get cool down there from time to time), so too lacy was not a good idea. Yet she didn't want it to be too chunky or too plain, because the project would be more fun if it was a challenge.

She liked retro-styling like the patterns found in the yarn books of the 1930s and has a collection started with purchases made on eBay. The garment had to at least come down to the forearms (from there the lap blanket can take over).

After conferring with her, I had a great idea for Buffie. I modified a circular shawl shape slightly. I was thinking in terms of a "shoulderetter"—basically a circle with a hole cut out in the middle for the head. Think of a yoked sweater without the sweater! Yet with a front opening, it's akin to a capelet.

I owe a great debt to Elizabeth Zimmermann (also known as EZ), one of knitting's independent pioneers. I followed EZ's formula for a yoke but worked from the top down instead. EZ had you decreasing to half the number of sts by the time you got halfway up, then decreasing to half the number of sts again another halfway up, like this: $\frac{1}{2}$ length = first dec, another $\frac{1}{4}$ length = second dec, another $\frac{1}{8}$ length = third decrease, etc.

Now, here's my trick for simplification with an ingenious decorative touch: On the rows where you have to *double* the number of sts (remember, it's neck-down), just go across and p 2, ★yarn over or wrap yarn around the needle in a purl-wise fashion, p 1; repeat from ★ending with p 2.

This is simple yet very effective. I'm particularly fond of things that are easy to do yet complex *looking*. This piece is also somewhat similar to EZ's "pi" shawl. It follows a similar principle of doubling the number of stitches when you double the number of rows.

Wearing a "doughnut" as a cape allows the back of the neck to droop down too far. To fill it in, I compensated for this within the neckband. The project begins with the neckband, worked from side to side. Stitches are increased as the piece progresses, to raise the back of the neck, and are decreased away again by the time the front of the neck is completed. Stitches are then picked up from this neckband and worked downward for the body.

Buffie and I had fun with combos of yarns. Using a simple eyelet pattern and a thin, lush silk/mohair yarn makes the shawl look light and airy, but it's still super warm. We added a separate color and texture of yarn to punctuate the ridges of the pattern. It met all of Buffie's requirements: lacy, but easy and not *too* lacy . . . and with texture to boot!

As you can see, this is a romantic piece. Very evocative of gothic New Orleans, no? I love the ethereal quality of the color in mohair.

Warning: When the piece comes off the needles, it looks ruffly and bunched up. To give it proper shape, blocking the piece is a must. Stretch it out on a flat surface, stick a gazillion pins to the edges, and get it real tight. I apply steam with a very good steam iron, but others have been known to liberally douse the whole piece with water and let it dry.

⟨·⟩ Instructions | Lace Capelet

Semicircular capelet worked from the top down

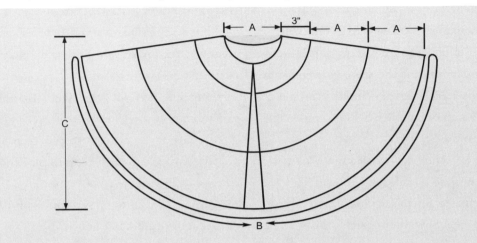

Finished Size: One size fits all.

Finished Measurements:

A. Neck width, either front or back = 6"

B. Circumference around outer edge = 56"

C. Total length = 18"

Materials:

- For Main Color (MC): K1C2 "Douceur et Soie" (70% baby mohair, 30% silk, 25g, appx 225yds/205m): 4 skeins color #8841 Fawn.
- For Contrast Color (CC): "Souffle" (70% viscose, 30% cotton, 50g, appx 104yds/95m): 2 skeins color #7111 Bavarian Creme.
- 24" circular knitting needles, size 6 or whatever size it

takes to get the gauge.

- Size 5 straight needles, or one size smaller than circulars used.
- Stitch markers.

Gauge: 18 sts and 36 rows = 4" in Ridged Lace pattern st on larger needles after steam blocking.

Special Notes: Two strands of Main Color are used together as one throughout. This is all worked in one piece from the top down, back-and-forth. Use the circular needles as if they were separate straight needles and work all parts back-and-forth to produce a flat piece. Carry color not in use very loosely along the side edge of work.

Ridged Lace Pattern Stitch

Pattern is worked over an odd number of sts.

Row 1, a Wrong Side row—with main color (MC), purl.

Row 2, a Right Side row—with MC, knit.

Row 3, eyelet row—with MC, p 1, *p 2 together, yo (wrap yarn around the needle in a purl-wise fashion); repeat from * to last 2 sts, end with p 2.

Row 4—with MC, knit.

Row 5—with MC, purl.

Row 6—switch to CC and knit.

Row 7—with CC, knit.

Row 8—switch to MC and knit.

Repeat Rows 1 through 8 for pattern.

Neck Band

With needles one size smaller than that used for gauge swatch and CC, cast on 3 sts.

Row 1—slip the first st as if to p with the yarn in front, bring yarn to the back, k 2.

Repeat Row 1 for Garter st with a slipped-st chain-selvedge (edge st) until 6 rows total have been worked.

Next row—slip the first st as if to p with the yarn in front, bring yarn to the back, increase in next st, k 1—4 sts.

Continue to work as for Row 1 on 4 sts for another 5 rows for 12 rows total.

Next row—slip the first st as if to p with the yarn in front, bring yarn to the back, increase in next st, k 2—5 sts.

Continue to work as for Row 1 on 5 sts for another 5 rows for 18 rows total.

Next row—slip the first st as if to p with the yarn in front, bring yarn to the back, increase in next st, k 3—6 sts.

Continue to work as for Row 1 on 6 sts for another 5 rows for 24 rows total.

Next row—slip the first st as if to p with the yarn in front, bring yarn to the back, increase in next st, k 4—7 sts.

Continue to work as for Row 1 on 7 sts for another 5 rows for 30 rows total.

Next row—slip the first st as if to p with the yarn in front, bring yarn to the back, increase in next st, k 5—8 sts.

Continue to work as for Row 1 on 8 sts for another 5 rows for 36 rows total.

Next row—slip the first st as if to p with the yarn in front, bring yarn to the back, increase in next st, k 6—9 sts.

Continue to work as for Row 1 on 9 sts for another 5 rows for 42 rows total.

Next row—slip the first st as if to p with the yarn in front, bring yarn to the back, increase in next st, k 7—10 sts.

Continue to work as for Row 1 on 10 sts for another 5 rows for 48 rows total.

Next row—slip the first st as if to p with the yarn in front, bring yarn to the back, increase in next st, k 8—11 sts.

Continue to work as for Row 1 on 11 sts for another 5 rows for 54 rows total.

Next row—slip the first st as if to p with the yarn in front, bring yarn to the back, increase in next st, k 9—12 sts.

Continue to work as for Row 1 on 12 sts for another 61 rows for 116 rows total.

■

Next row—slip the first st as if to p with the yarn in front, bring yarn to the back, k the next 2 sts together (k2tog) for a decrease, k 9—11 sts.

Continue to work as for Row 1 on 11 sts for another 5 rows for 122 rows total.

Next row—slip the first st as if to p with the yarn in front, bring yarn to the back, k2tog for a decrease, k 8—10 sts.

Continue to work as for Row 1 on 10 sts for another 5 rows for 128 rows total.

Next row—slip the first st as if to p with the yarn in front, bring yarn to the back, k2tog for a decrease, k 7—9 sts.

Continue to work as for Row 1 on 9 sts for another 5 rows for 134 rows total.

Next row—slip the first st as if to p with the yarn in front, bring yarn to the back, k2tog for a decrease, k 6—8 sts.

Continue to work as for Row 1 on 8 sts for another 5 rows for 140 rows total.

Next row—slip the first st as if to p with the yarn in front, bring yarn to the back, k2tog for a decrease, k 5—7 sts.

Continue to work as for Row 1 on 7 sts for another 5 rows for 146 rows total.

Next row—slip the first st as if to p with the yarn in front, bring yarn to the back, k2tog for a decrease, k 4—6 sts.

Continue to work as for Row 1 to 6 sts for another 5 rows for 152 rows total.

Next row—slip the first st as if to p with the yarn in front, bring yarn to the back, k2tog for a decrease, k 3—5 sts.

Continue to work as for Row 1 on 5 sts for another 5 rows for 158 rows total.

Next row—slip the first st as if to p with the yarn in front, bring yarn to the back, k2tog for a decrease, k 2—4 sts.

Continue to work as for Row 1 on 4 sts for another 5 rows for 164 rows total.

Next row—slip the first st as if to p with the yarn in front, bring yarn to the back, k2tog for a decrease, k1—3 sts.

Continue to work Row 1 on 3 sts for another 4 rows for 169 rows total. Bind off in knit on next row, do not end off yarn.

Body

With larger circular needles and *double strand* of Main Color (MC), begin where other yarn ended. Pick up and knit 1 st for every 2 rows (pick up 1 st for each "chain loop" formed by the slipped sts) across the curved edge of neck band—85 sts.

Begin Row 1 of Ridged Lace pattern st and continue in the Ridged Lace pattern st until 26 rows total of pattern have been worked (there are 3 CC ridges), ending with Row 2 of pattern.

Next row [an Increase row], Wrong Side faces you—p 2, yo, ★p 1, yo, repeat from ★, end with p 2—167 sts.

Continue in Ridged Lace pattern beginning with Row 4 of pattern and work until 82 rows total of pattern have been worked (there are 10 CC ridges), ending with Row 2 of pattern.

Repeat the Increase row on Wrong Side—331 sts.

Continue in Ridged Lace pattern beginning with Row 4 of pattern and work until piece measures about 15" from beginning pick-up row or to desired length, ending with Row 7 of pattern, end off MC. Bind off very loosely in knit with CC on next Right Side row but do not end off yarn.

Trim

With Right Side facing you, remaining CC, and circular needles, begin at bottom and pick up and knit evenly along right front edge (about every other row) to top of neck band, cast on 54 sts for tie, turn work.

Next row, a Wrong Side row—slip the first st as if to p with the yarn in front, bring yarn to the back, k to end.

Bind off in knit on next Right Side row, end off yarn. Cast on 54 sts with CC onto circular needles for tie, then with Right Side facing you, begin at top of neck band. Pick up and knit evenly along left front edge (about every other row) to bottom edge, turn work.

Next row, a Wrong Side row—slip the first st as if to p with the yarn in front, bring yarn to the back, k to end.

Bind off in knit on next Right Side row, end off yarn.

Finishing

Steam block piece to smooth and even out. It is very important to stretch to measurements and let dry to prevent ruffling.

Cardi-Jacket | Sarah Poriss

Lily M. Chin

CITY: Hartford, CT
AGE: 31

Sarah is a law student at the University of Connecticut School of Law, a community gardener, dog lover, speed skater, and knitter. She grew up in a suburb of Hartford and has been living within the city limits since May 1997. She studies the details of the Victorian homes in her neighborhood as she walks the half mile to the school's campus. The Bright Orange Hat that keeps her warm on her walk is recognized by many (She was in a crowd of people on a local news report and several friends and relatives said they could pick her out by her hat!).

Her mother taught her to cast on, knit, and purl at around age eleven, but neither one of them ever completed any real garments. In Maine in 1993, a post-college roommate of Sarah's taught her how to make socks. Knitting socks gave Sarah the skills and confidence to tackle sweaters and other items. Sarah's been a yarnaholic ever since, especially after joining the KnitList on the Internet in December 1998.

Inspiration

Sarah doesn't like to stand out in a crowd, but at the same time does not want to wear what everyone else wears. That's why she likes mellow colors—maroon, browns, blues, greens, grays, all in solids. Stripes make her self-conscious! She likes a vintage look and is glad that styles from the 1920s through the '70s have come back and are being streamlined into a modern look. That gets her imagination going and gives her many "looks" to base designs on.

Since entering the field of law, she's been faced with the reality that she'll have to wear suits the rest of her life. The cost of tuition means she has a limited budget, and good jackets are not cheap. She is dismayed that every time there is a professional affair on campus (like the Career Fair or a Law Review forum), everyone wears a black suit, men and women alike. She wants to cry, "Get some individuality, will you? Just because you are expected to dress formally in court and for clients does not mean you have to wear black suits!"

While watching *Law and Order* and similar television shows, she noticed that the women lawyers/professionals were wearing suits with original styling (or else they'd all look alike). This was what she wanted to design—a knit jacket that qualifies for formal occasions but does not make her feel like she's trying to "dress like a man."

Fit and finishing are important to Sarah. She wanted her item not to look crafty or grandmotherly. She sent me a rough sketch of what she had in mind. I immediately adored her idea of using ribbing to give her jacket shape.

Rather than having one ribbed band across the middle of the jacket where the waist is, we judiciously place them at the lower back and below each bust-point. This way there is no horizontal line breaking up the overall clean effect, yet there is a great shape within.

So that the lower edge doesn't pull in like the ribbing on a cardigan sweater, I had Sarah cast on many more stitches to achieve the same width in ribbing as the Stockinette portion above it. She then decreased the extra stitches away when beginning Stockinette.

Adding a collar is a must, but it is an easy pick-up from a shallow V-neck. The piece is then worked straight. Instead of a full sleeve cap, which gives many knitters fits when the time comes to set them in properly, I opted for a much simpler angled armhole. It is still quite refined and fitted but much easier to do. Leather buttons finish off this tailored look.

As with several of the other projects in this book, fully fashioned decreases are important to this polished look. They show off the shaping and announce that thought and care were taken in the making of the garment. This, too, met another of Sarah's demands.

Sarah stipulated muted business-professional colors and the heathered oxford gray is right up her alley. However, as lovely as the smooth, worsted merino wool is, adding a touch of carry-along, thin lace-weight mohair created a texture that really made the jacket come alive! It met another of Sarah's criteria by making the jacket more unique, with just enough of a halo fuzzing up the surface.

This jacket almost reminds me of the 1920s-style Gatsby look, a nod to the vintage styling Sarah was after. It may not be a giant step away from formal suit requirements, but it has definite feminine shaping and a sensuous fabric.

Instructions | Cardi-Jacket

Standard/relaxed fitting with angled-in sleeves

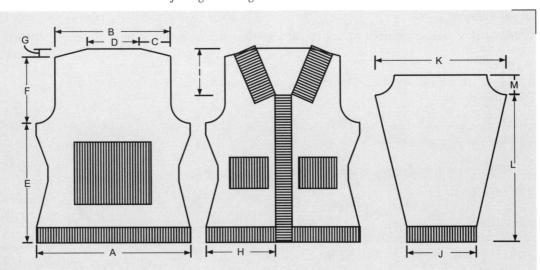

Finished Size: Garment measures 36 (40, 44)" at bust and is 24.5 (25, 25.5)" long.

Finished Measurements: (Do not include selvedges of 1 st at each end.)

- **A.** Back bottom and bust = 18 (20, 22)"
- **B.** Across shoulders = 14 (15, 16)"
- **C.** Each shoulder width = 3.5 (4, 4.5)"
- **D.** Neck width = 7"
- **E.** Body length = 15.5"
- **F.** Armhole length = 8 (8.5, 9)"
- **G.** Shoulder slope = 1"
- **H.** Half front width = 8 (9, 10)"
- **I.** Front neck depth = 6"
- **J.** Sleeve width at bottom = 8 (9, 10)"
- **K.** Sleeve width at top = 16 (17, 18)"
- **L.** Sleeve length to underarm = 19"
- **M.** Sleeve "cap" = 2 (2.5, 3)"

Materials:

- Karabella "Aurora 8" (100% merino wool, 50g, appx 98yds): 14 (15, 17) skeins #26 Pewter.
- Karabella "Lace Mohair" (61% kid mohair, 8% wool, 31% polyamid, 50g, appx 540yds): 3 skeins #172 Smoke Melange.
- Size 6 knitting needles, or whatever size it takes to get the gauge.
- Six 7/8" leather buttons.
- Stitch markers.

Gauge: 20 sts and 28 rows = 4" in Stockinette st.

Special Notes: Always work with a strand of each yarn held together as one.

Slip-slip-knit is described on page 25.

Back

Cast on 122 (134, 146) sts. Work 2 × 2 Ribbing as follows:

Row 1 or the Right Side (RS)—★k 2 and p 2; repeat from ★ across, then end with k 2.

Row 2 or the Wrong Side (WS)—★p 2 and k 2; repeat from ★ across, then end with p 2.

Repeat Rows 1 and 2 until work measures 2", end by finishing a WS row.

Next row or the RS—★k 2, k next 2 purl sts together; repeat from ★ 29 (15, 16) more times; there are 2 (70, 78) sts remaining on the left needle still to be worked, k the next 2 (6, 10) sts.

Sizes 40 and 44 *only*: ★k the next 2 purl sts together, k 2; repeat from ★ to end of row.

There are now 92 (102, 112) sts total.

Begin Stockinette st [p the WS rows and k the RS rows] and work until piece measures 5" total, end by finishing a WS row as follows: p 21 (26, 31), place a st marker onto the needle, p another 50, place another st marker onto the needle, p the remaining 21 (26, 31) sts. From here on, just slip the st markers as you work [they're there to keep your place].

Shape waist:

Next row or the RS—k up to the first st marker, ★p 2, k 2; repeat from ★ up to the next st marker ending with a p 2; k remainder of sts.

From here on, keep the Stockinette sts in Stockinette and the newly begun 2 × 2 Ribbing in Ribbing and work until piece measures 13" from beginning (measure the Stockinette portion for height).

Switch back to all Stockinette st again while removing the st markers in the process.

Work until piece measures 15.5" from beginning, end with a p row.

Shape armholes:

Bind off 4 (5, 6) sts at the beginning of the next RS row—88 (97, 106) sts remain.

Bind off 4 (5, 6) sts at the beginning of the next WS row—84 (92, 100) sts remain.

Next row or the RS—k 2, k the next 2 sts together, k to last 4 sts, slip-slip-knit the next 2 sts together, k last 2 sts—82 (90, 98) sts remain.

Next row or the WS—p across.

Repeat the last 2 rows 5 (7, 8) times; there will be 2 less sts after each RS row worked. There are 72 (76, 82) sts remaining after the last repeat.

Continue in Stockinette st until piece measures 23.5 (24, 24.5)" total [measure the Stockinette portion for height] or 8 (8.5, 9)" from the beginning of the armhole shaping, ending with a p row.

Shape shoulders:

Bind off 4 sts at the beginning of the next 4 (8, 2) rows, then bind off 3 (0, 5) sts at the beginning of the next 4 (0, 6) rows. Bind off the remaining 44 sts.

Right Front

Cast on 54 (62, 66) sts. Work 2 × 2 Ribbing as for back for 2", end by finishing a WS row.

Next row or the RS—k 6 (2, 6), ★k next 2 purl sts together, k 2; repeat from ★ 11 (14, 13) more times, end with k 0 (0, 4). There are now 42 (47, 52) sts total.

Begin Stockinette st [p the WS rows and k the RS rows] and work until piece measures 7" total, end by finishing a WS row as follows: p 14 (19, 24), place a st marker onto the needle, p another 22, place another st marker onto the needle, p the remaining 6 sts. From here on, just slip the st markers as you work [they're there to keep your place].

Shape waist:

Next row or the RS—k up to the first st marker, ★p 2, k 2; repeat from ★ up to the next st marker, ending with a p 2; k remainder of sts.

From here on, keep the Stockinette sts in Stockinette and the newly begun 2 × 2 Ribbing in Ribbing and work until piece measures 11" (measure the Stockinette portion for height).

Switch back to all Stockinette st again while removing the st markers in the process. Work until piece measures 15.5", end with a k row.

Shape armholes:

Bind off 4 (5, 6) sts at the beginning of the next WS row—38 (42, 46) sts remain.

Next row or the RS—k to last 4 sts, slip-slip-knit the next 2 sts together, k last 2 sts—37 (41, 45) sts remain.

Next row or the WS—p across.

Repeat the last 2 rows 5 (7, 8) times; there will be 1 less st after each RS row worked. There are 32 (34, 37) sts remaining after the last repeat.

Continue in Stockinette st until piece measures 18.5 (19, 19.5)" total or 3 (3.5, 4)" from the beginning of the armhole shaping, end with a p row. Mark the end of this row with a little piece of scrap yarn or a safety pin.

Shape front neck:

★Next row or the RS [a Decrease row]—k 2, k 2 together, k remainder of sts.

P one row, k one row, p one row. Repeat the Decrease row. P one row. Continue to repeat the last 6 rows [or repeat from ★] another 6 times, and at the same time, when piece measures 23.5 (24, 24.5)" total [measure the Stockinette portion for height] or 8 (8.5, 9)" from the beginning of the armhole shaping, end with a p row, and begin to shape shoulders.

Shape shoulders:

Still continuing the decreases at the neck edge, bind off 4 sts at the beginning of the next row [this is the shoulder edge]. Bind off 4 (4, 5) sts at this shoulder edge every WS row another 1 (3, 3) times, then bind off 3 (0, 0) sts another 2 times. Bind off the remaining 4 sts, end off.

Left Front

Work the bottom Ribbing same as for the right front but reverse the decreasing. Beg Stockinette st [p the WS rows and k the RS rows] and work until piece measures 7" total, end by finishing a WS row as follows: p 6, place a st marker onto the needle, p another 22, place another st marker onto the needle, p the remaining 14 (19, 24) sts. From here on, just slip the st markers as you work [they're there to keep your place].

Shape waist:

Next row or the RS—k up to the first st marker, *p 2, k 2; repeat from * up to the next st marker, ending with a p 2; k remainder of sts.

From here on, keep the Stockinette sts in Stockinette and the newly begun 2 × 2 Ribbing in Ribbing and work until piece measures 11" (measure the Stockinette portion for height).

Switch back to all Stockinette st again while removing the st markers in the process. Work until piece measures 15.5", end with a p row.

Shape armholes:

Bind off 4 (5, 6) sts at the beginning of the next RS row—38 (42, 46) sts remain. P one row.

Next row or the RS—k 2, knit the next 2 sts together, k to the end—37 (41, 45) sts remain.

Next row or the WS—p across.

Repeat the last 2 rows 5 (7, 8) times, there will be 1 less st after each RS row worked. There are 32 (34, 37) sts remaining after the last repeat.

Continue in Stockinette st until piece measures 18.5 (19, 19.5)" total or 3 (3.5, 4)" from the beginning of the armhole shaping, end with a p row. Mark the beginning of this row with a little piece of scrap yarn or a safety pin.

Shape front neck:

*Next row or the RS [a Decrease row]—k to the last 4 sts, slip-slip-knit the next 2 sts together, k the last 2 sts.

P one row, k one row, p one row. Repeat the Decrease row. P one row. Continue to repeat the last 6 rows [or repeat from *] another 6 times, and at the same time, when piece measures 23.5 (24, 24.5)" total (measure the Stockinette portion for height) or 8 (8.5, 9)" from the beginning of the armhole shaping, end with a p row, and begin to shape shoulders.

Shape shoulders:

Still continuing the decreases at the neck edge, bind off 4 sts at the beginning of the next row [this is the shoulder edge]. Bind off 4 (4, 5) sts at this shoulder edge every RS row another 1 (3, 3) times, then bind off 3 (0, 0) sts another 2 times. Bind off the remaining 4 sts, end off.

Sleeves (Make 2)

Cast on 54 (62, 66) sts. Work 2 × 2 Ribbing as for back for 2", end by finishing a WS row.

Next row or the RS—k 6 (2, 6), ★k next 2 purl sts together, k 2; repeat from ★ 11 (14, 13) more times, end with k 0 (0, 4). There are now 42 (47, 52) sts total.

Begin Stockinette st [p the WS rows and k the RS rows] and on the next RS row, increase 1 st at each edge as follows: k 2, make 1 increase, k to the last 2 sts, make another increase, k the last 2 sts. Work this increase row in same manner every 6th row another 19 times total. Work even on 82 (87, 92) sts until sleeve measures 19" from the beginning.

Shape "cap":

Bind off 4 (5, 6) sts at the beginning of the next RS row—78 (82, 86) sts remain.

Bind off 4 (5, 6) sts at the beginning of the next WS row—74 (77, 80) sts remain.

Next row or the RS—k 2, k the next 2 sts together, k to last 4 sts, slip-slip-knit the next 2 sts together, k last 2 sts—72 (75, 78) sts remain.

Next row or the WS—p across.

Repeat the last 2 rows 5 (7, 8) times; there will be 2 less sts after each RS row worked. There are 62 (61, 62) sts remaining after the last repeat.

Bind off.

Finishing

Block pieces to measurements. Sew shoulder seams.

Button band:

With RS facing you, begin at marker at base of left front neck. Pick up and k 114 (118, 122) sts evenly spaced along center edge of left front to the bottom [about 1 st for each row]. Work 2 × 2 Ribbing as for back for 2"; bind off in Ribbing. Mark for 6 buttons evenly spaced with the top one close to the top edge; bottom one can be as close or as far from bottom edge as desired. Try to place buttons in the p-2 indents of Ribbing.

Buttonhole band:

With RS facing you, begin at bottom edge. Pick up and k 114 (118, 122) sts evenly spaced along center edge of right front to the marker at bottom of right front neck [about 1 st for each row]. Work 2 × 2 Ribbing as for back for 1". Work buttonholes to correspond to marked buttons of left front as follows: ★ work Ribbing to first marker, bind off 2 sts; repeat from ★ across. On next row, cast on 2 sts for each of the 2 bound-off sts of previous row. When band measures 2", bind off in Ribbing.

Collar:

With RS facing you, begin at marker at bottom of right front neck. Pick up and k 44 sts evenly spaced up neck edge [about 1 st for each row] and 38 sts evenly spaced across back neck and 44 sts down left front neck [about 1 st for each row] to other marker—126 sts. Work 2 × 2 Ribbing as for back for 3.5"; bind off in Ribbing.

■

Set in sleeves. Sew side and sleeve seams. Sew buttons opposite buttonholes.

Lattice Pullover | Tara Weinstein

Lily M. Chin

CITY: Providence, RI
AGE: 23

Tara is originally from Toronto, Ontario, Canada. She's soon to be married and teaches physics at a private high school in Providence. She has a degree in engineering and another one in education.

Tara started knitting when she was twenty. She was flipping through an L.L. Bean catalog and saw a sweater that she thought was nice, but too expensive. Having no concept of yarn prices, she was quite sure that if she learned how to knit, she could make the same sweater for much less. The next day she went to the store and bought a pattern, yarn, and a learn-to-knit book. The very first thing she knit was the gauge swatch for a sweater. The second thing was the sweater itself, a drop-shouldered, basket-weave turtleneck. Her second project was an allover cabled sweater using a mohair blend. No one had told her that she shouldn't start with these projects, so she didn't realize that they were supposed to be too advanced. Of course, if someone *had* told her, she says she probably would have taken it as a challenge ("Sometimes I'm a little too obstinate for my own good").

Even though she thinks it's important to feature some simple items in this book, there should also be other projects that present more of a challenge and perhaps more of an inspiration to prospective knitters. Of course, not everyone is as intrepid as Tara. She started sewing a couple of years ago because she was going to be graduating from college and needed a suit for interviews, but couldn't afford to buy one—so she made one!

Inspiration

For Tara, a toasty woolen pullover with cabled textures was called for, since this was what she had done as her first knitting project. In order for cabled textures to show boldly, we wanted a smooth yarn. The llama/wool blend we chose is heavy-worsted and that touch of luxury makes a wardrobe basic more special. Since texture was so important, lighter colors were within our palette. Most cabled sweaters are warm cream, so I liked the idea of using a cool gray instead. We could easily have used a light blue or teal to break away from the traditional. If you really want to get bold, try lime green or even magenta. It would be shocking but the stitchery will show up dramatically.

Tara wondered about the feel of the yarn. At first, the skein felt a little scratchy. With washing, however, it softened up. This is true of any animal fiber. Handling the project in progress also softens it. Besides, this style is suited as an over-layer. With a loose fit, it may be layered over something else, like a cotton turtleneck.

Tara and I reviewed a few stitch dictionaries together to decide on a cable pattern. We avoided overly intricate patterns with very large stitch and/or row repeats. In an allover cable pattern, I was concerned about how to accommodate the shaping. Even if the armhole is a straight bind-off, I needed to figure out how to shape the neck.

One way to deal with this might be to do only a cabled center panel, not quite neck's width, for the front and back, and about the wrist's width for sleeves. Then the sides can be a filler Moss or Seed or Double-Moss or even plain Reverse Stockinette or just Garter (provided the row gauge is relatively the same as the cable pattern). The shaping of the sleeves could then be done in these plainer areas. The neck could be a bind-off of the fancy cable first, all at once, then shaped with decreases in the plain areas.

Tara's original plan called for stitches to be bound off/decreased in some multiple of the pattern repeat. She'd bind off some of those, and work the rest in Reverse Stockinette until they were decreased away. The same approach would apply to sleeve increases—working all increased stitches as background until there were enough to start another pattern repeat. She adapts all patterns like this.

I warned her that one thing to look out for is too large a repeat. If it's a loooong way before you get enough stitches for another repeat, it can look very jarring to—*boom*—suddenly find another big pattern pop in. Also, from a gauge point of view, since cables draw in more than, say, Reverse Stockinette, the loooong stretches can poof out awkwardly before you get a chance to draw them back in to begin a new cable. Thus, I thought Tara's strategy more successful in smaller pattern repeats.

The pattern we decided on is a 26-stitch repeat. For the neck, try to keep to pattern as much as possible while working the decrease-shaping. As for the sleeves, Tara had to relent and keep the side stitches in Reverse Stockinette.

Blocking is an important aspect of *any* project, but this is especially true of cables. Only when the swatch is blocked do you know your true gauge because of the highly textural nature of this fabric.

Cables are warm because the fabric is thickened. Tara and I agreed that a straight-hanging tunic style tends to be more flattering without the bulge-out effect over a pull-in ribbed band. As with several other projects in this book, adding 2 Stockinette selvedge stitches on each side allows for easier and neater seaming (and picking up of stitches) at the end. Since there's Reverse Stockinette at the sides of the sleeves, I thought a small inward-roll of the same as a neck trim looked better than the ubiquitous rib. The squared-off armholes are a less-bulky alternative to drop-shoulders, yet are easy to do and quite flattering.

Instructions | Lattice Pullover

Loose-fitting cabled pullover with square-inset sleeves

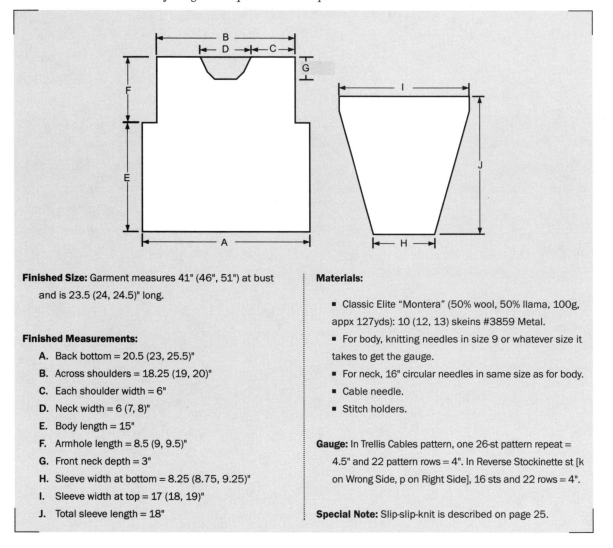

Finished Size: Garment measures 41" (46", 51") at bust and is 23.5 (24, 24.5)" long.

Finished Measurements:

- **A.** Back bottom = 20.5 (23, 25.5)"
- **B.** Across shoulders = 18.25 (19, 20)"
- **C.** Each shoulder width = 6"
- **D.** Neck width = 6 (7, 8)"
- **E.** Body length = 15"
- **F.** Armhole length = 8.5 (9, 9.5)"
- **G.** Front neck depth = 3"
- **H.** Sleeve width at bottom = 8.25 (8.75, 9.25)"
- **I.** Sleeve width at top = 17 (18, 19)"
- **J.** Total sleeve length = 18"

Materials:

- Classic Elite "Montera" (50% wool, 50% llama, 100g, appx 127yds): 10 (12, 13) skeins #3859 Metal.
- For body, knitting needles in size 9 or whatever size it takes to get the gauge.
- For neck, 16" circular needles in same size as for body.
- Cable needle.
- Stitch holders.

Gauge: In Trellis Cables pattern, one 26-st pattern repeat = 4.5" and 22 pattern rows = 4". In Reverse Stockinette st [k on Wrong Side, p on Right Side], 16 sts and 22 rows = 4".

Special Note: Slip-slip-knit is described on page 25.

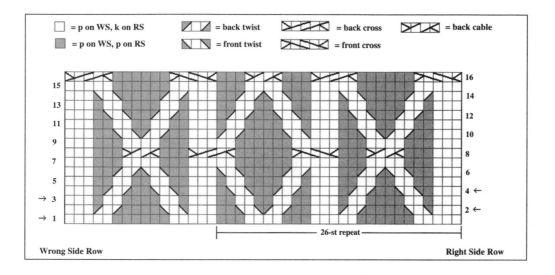

| | = p on WS, k on RS | | = back twist | | = back cross | | = back cable |
| | = p on WS, p on RS | | = front twist | | = front cross | | |

Wrong Side Row

26-st repeat

Right Side Row

Trellis Cables Pattern

Pattern is a multiple of 26 sts plus 16 extra.

Row 1 [Wrong Side]—p 5, k 6, p 5, ★k 3, p 4, k 3, p 5, k 6, p 5; repeat from ★ to end.

Row 2 [Right Side]—★k 3, (slip 2 sts to cable needle, hold to front of work, p 1, k 2 from cable needle) = front twist, p 4, (slip 1 st to cable needle, hold to back of work, k 2, p 1 from cable needle) = back twist, k 3, p 2, back twist, front twist, p 2; repeat from ★; end k 3, front twist, p 4, back twist, k 3.

Row 3—p 3, k 1, p 2, k 4, p 2, k 1, p 3, ★k 2, [p 2, k 2] twice, p 3, k 1, p 2, k 4, p 2, k 1, p 3; repeat from ★ to end.

Basically, *all Wrong Side rows or odd-numbered rows* are: k the k sts and p the p sts as they face you.

Row 4—★k 3, p 1, front twist, p 2, back twist, p 1, k 3, p 1, back twist, p 2, front twist, p 1; repeat from ★; end k 3, p 1, front twist, p 2, back twist, p 1, k 3.

Row 5—p 3, k 2, [p 2, k 2] twice, p 3, ★k 1, p 2, k 4, p 2, k 1, p 3, k 2, [p 2, k 2] twice, p 3; repeat from ★ to end.

Row 6—★k 3, p 2, front twist, back twist, p 2, k 3, back twist, p 4, front twist; repeat from ★; end k 3, p 2, front twist, back twist, p 2, k 3.

Row 7—p 3, k 3, p 4, k 3, p 3, ★p 2, k 6, p 5, k 3, p 4, k 3, p 3; repeat from ★ to end.

Row 8—k 3, ★p 3, (slip 2 sts to cable needle, hold at back of work, k 2, k 2 from cable needle) = back cable, p 3, (slip 2 sts to cable needle, hold at front of work, k 3, k 2 from cable needle) =

front cross, p 6, (slip 3 sts to cable needle, hold at back of work, k 2, k 3 from cable needle) = back cross; repeat from ★; end p 3, back cable, p 3, k 3.

Row 9—work as for Row 7.

Row 10—★k 3, p 2, back twist, front twist, p 2, k 3, front twist, p 4, back twist; repeat from ★; end k 3, p 2, back twist, front twist, p 2, k 3.

Row 11—work as for Row 5.

Row 12—★k 3, p 1, back twist, p 2, front twist, p 1, k 3, p 1, front twist, p 2, back twist, p 1; repeat from ★; end k 3, p 1, back twist, p 2, front twist, p 1, k 3.

Row 13—work as for Row 3.

Row 14—★k 3, back twist, p 4, front twist, k 3, p 2, front twist, back twist, p 2; repeat from ★; end k 3, back twist, p 4, front twist, k 3.

Row 15—work as for Row 1.

Row 16—★front cross, p 6, back cross, p 3, back cable, p 3; repeat from ★; end front cross, p 6, back cross.

Repeat Rows 1 through 16 for pattern.

Back

Cast on 124 (132, 150) sts.

Row 1 [Wrong Side]—p 2, k 0 (4, 0), work 120 (120, 146) sts in Row 1 of Trellis Cables pattern, k 0 (4, 0), p 2

Row 2 [Right Side]—k 2, p 0 (4, 0), work 120 (120, 146) sts in Row 2 of Trellis Cables pattern, p 0 (4, 0), k 2.

Row 3—p 2, k 0 (4, 0), work 120 (120, 146) sts in Row 3 of Trellis Cables pattern, k 0 (4, 0), p 2.

Row 4—k 2, p 0 (4, 0), work 120 (120, 146) sts in Row 4 of Trellis Cables pattern, p 0 (4, 0), k 2.

Continue in this manner until the back measures 15" from beginning.

Armholes:

Bind off first 8 (10, 16) sts of next two rows—108 (112, 118) sts.

Continue the pattern as established but maintain first 2 and last 2 sts in Stockinette (k on Right Side rows, p on Wrong Side rows]. Work until the armholes measure 8.5 (9, 9.5)".

Shoulders:

Bind off 36 sts at the beginning of the next two rows. Put the remaining 36 (40, 46) sts on a stitch holder.

Front

Work as back until the armholes measure 5.5 (6, 6.5)", end with a Right Side row.

Neck:

Work 43 (43, 44) sts in established pattern. Put center 22 (26, 30) sts on stitch holder. Attach a new ball of yarn and work the last 43 (43, 44) sts in established pattern. Work both sides of neck simultaneously.

Next row [Right Side]—work to last 4 sts before neck in established pattern. K 2 together to decrease, k 2. On other side of neck, k 2, slip-slip-knit decrease, work remaining sts in established pattern.

Next row [Wrong Side]—work sts in established pattern.

Repeat these 2 rows 6 (6, 7) more times, so that they will have been worked a total of 7 (7, 8) times. Continue without decreasing any further sts until total armhole depth is 8.5 (9, 9.5)". Bind off all sts.

Sleeves

Cast on 48 (50, 52) sts.

Row 1 [Wrong Side]—p 2, k 1 (2, 3), work 42 sts in Row 1 of Trellis Cables pattern, k 1 (2, 3), p 2.

Row 2 [Right Side]—k 2, p 1 (2, 3), work 42 sts in Row 2 of Trellis Cables pattern, p 1 (2, 3), k 2.

Row 3—p 2, k 1 (2, 3), work 42 sts in Row 3 of Trellis Cables pattern, k 1 (2, 3), p 2.

Row 4—k 2, p 1 (2, 3), work 42 sts in Row 4 of Trellis Cables pattern, p 1 (2, 3), k 2.

Continue in the pattern as established, increasing 1 st at each end after first 2 and before last 2 Stockinette sts on next row, then every 5th (4th, 4th) row 18 (19, 20) times total. Keep the increased sts in Reverse Stockinette.

Work even on 84 (88, 92) sts until sleeve measures 18". Bind off.

Finishing

Block pieces to measurements. Sew shoulder seams. Set in sleeves by sewing tops of sleeves to straight part of armholes, then sew straight portion at tops of sleeves to bound-off armhole sts. Sew side and sleeve seams.

Collar:

On circular needles, with Right Side facing you, p 36 (40, 46) sts from back neck holder, pick up and k 12 sts along left neck edge, p 22 (26, 30) sts from front neck holder, pick up and k 12 sts along right neck edge. Place a st marker onto needle to mark beginning/end of rounds. Working circularly [in the round] with Right Side always facing you, p all 82 (90, 100) sts for 4 rows. Loosely bind off all sts around.

Unisex Garter-Striped Diagonal Vest

Tony Ching

CITY: San Francisco, CA
AGE: 34

Lily M. Chin

Tony works in the public service department of a medical society. When he's not volunteering to run a users' group on handheld computing, he enjoys triaxial weaving, making paper Buddhas, and of course knitting! He knits with the yarn around his neck as people in the Andes and parts of Europe do. He enjoys making sweaters that are puzzles of design.

Tony started knitting in 1987 after he fell in love with an Aran sweater his then-girlfriend Barbara was wearing. She taught him the fundamentals and exposed him to the virtues of the cable cast-on. Her Irish background, coupled with the romance of Aran knitting, enticed him to clothe himself in rich tradition and symbolism. He was bitten by the ethnography bug and immersed himself in a cultural review of knitting. From knitting, he discovered weaving and other fiber crafts and proceeded to learn everything he could.

Sometimes knitting can be a passion for Tony. He writes, "The direct immediacy of knitting, the rhythm of stitches forming an ocean of shaped patterns and form, is a source of endless fascination for me. The knitter is a matchmaker of form and function. The modern world underestimates the value of the hand. Modern clothes are spit out by machine or mass labors. Knitting is a small oasis. Knitting is ritual. It's a creative rebellion; a yearning to break free of the unseen mold that surrounds us. When the light fades and time ceases, you can't get enough. It's your fix. Row by row, pattern block by block, you need it. Mind moving hands, hands molding mind. . . ."

Knitting was coming back in style in the early 1990s at the time the Internet was emerging from its university setting. Tony joined a community on the Internet called the KnitList while studying nursing in graduate school (he is now a registered nurse). It was online that he "met" me and initiated the witty repartee between us that continues today. Tony flatteringly proclaims, "Master knitter Lily Chin has been my knit mentor and hero ever since." I like anyone who calls me "master."

Inspiration

This vest bridges a bit of Tony's knitting past and future. He says, "There is a vast difference between having the seed of your ideal creation and actually implementing it. I had a strong image and desire to create this 'quick 'n' easy' master-piece, but it took Lily's vast experience and follow-through to help bring this vest to life.

"Why a vest? In addition to Lily, this vest is also dedicated to Lun Po. Lun Po was a dear friend of my grandmother's. My first exposure to knitting was at the age of four. I remember receiving many gaudy hunter orange acrylic vests lovingly created by her skillful hands. This remarkable woman would knit me intricately formed armor about every Chinese New Year. The sight of little boys in these utilitarian vests serves as a cultural vestige even today. It is common to see Chinese grannies carrying bundled infants on their backs while completing the ensemble with these vests or other garments.

"At heart, I'm still a little boy. I wanted a garment that is versatile, that I could wear with a nice dress shirt or over polar fleece. I could pick it up and wear it all the time. For a working stiff, it had to be quick and easy to make."

Tony is a native San Franciscan, named by his mom after the TV hunk Anthony Franciosa. It was a good thing, as he was raised in San Francisco's Chinatown right next to the city's famed Italian district, North Beach. San Francisco is a great mix of cultures, and the design of this vest reflects a bit of that blending for Tony. The bold striped patterning is reminiscent of Andean mantles from the Late Intermediate Period. The bias slant comes from the great creative fashion designers of Japan. To Tony, these two cultures represent the best in textile tradition. He wanted to combine the Andean past with a Japanese future. This coupling of bias and rhythmic striping has an instant appeal and reflects an intelligent flair. The yarn we chose had great colors to realize this somewhat ethnic look. It also feels wonderful as it's a blend of mohair and wool.

I turned him on to Garter stitch, as a quick and happy medium for this design, by providing him with my notes for a class I teach on bias knitting. He says, "This vest illustrates the art and science of knitting."

Instructions | Unisex Garter-Striped Diagonal Vest

Standard-fitting vest worked from corner to corner

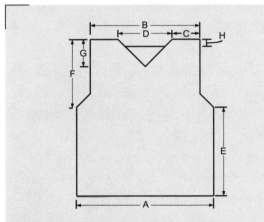

Finished Size: Small (Medium, Large). Garment measures 38 (40, 42)" at the chest and is 22 (23, 24)" long.

Finished Measurements:
A. Back/front bottom width = 19 (20, 21)"
B. Across shoulders = 15 (16, 17)"
C. Each shoulder width = 3.75 (4, 4.25)"
D. Neck width = 7.5 (8, 8.5)"
E. Body length = 12 (13, 13.5)"
F. Armhole length = 10 (10, 10.5)"
G. Front neck depth = 4 (4, 4.25)"
H. Back neck depth = 2"

Materials:
- Kertzer/Naturally "Karen M Luxury Double Knit" (50% wool, 50% mohair, 50g, appx 104m/113yds): 2 (3, 3) skeins each of the following colors—#936 Blue (color A), #933 Red (color B), and #994 Gold (color C)—and 3 (3, 4) skeins of #996 Black (color D).
- For body, size 5 knitting needles, or whatever size it takes to get the gauge.
- For trim, double-pointed knitting needles of the same size as for body.

Gauge: 18 sts and 36 rows = 4" in Garter st.

Stitch Pattern

Garter stitch [knit all rows].

1 garter stitch ridge = 2 rows of knitting.

Color Pattern

Four colors: A, B, C, and D.

Band 1: Work 4 rows of C, 2 rows of A, then 4 rows of C for 2 ridges C, 1 ridge A, 2 ridges C.

Band 2: Work 4 rows of D, 2 rows of B, then 4 rows of D for 2 ridges D, 1 ridge B, 2 ridges D.

Band 3: Work 4 rows of A, 2 rows of C, then 4 rows of A for 2 ridges A, 1 ridge C, 2 ridges A.

Band 4: Work 4 rows of B, 2 rows of D, then 4 rows of B for 2 ridges B, 1 ridge D, 2 ridges B.

Band 5: Work 4 rows of C, 2 rows of B, then 4 rows of C for 2 ridges C, 1 ridge B, 2 ridges C.

Band 6: Work 4 rows of D, 2 rows of A, then 4 rows of D for 2 ridges D, 1 ridge A, 2 ridges D.

Band 7: Work 4 rows of B, 2 rows of C, then 4 rows of B for 2 ridges B, 1 ridge C, 2 ridges B.

Band 8: Work 4 rows of A, 2 rows of D, then 4 rows of A for 2 ridges A, 1 ridge D, 2 ridges A.

Band 9: Work 4 rows of D, 2 rows of C, then 4 rows of D for 2 ridges D, 1 ridge C, 2 ridges D.

Band 10: Work 4 rows of B, 2 rows of A, then 4 rows of B for 2 ridges B, 1 ridge A, 2 ridges B.

Band 11: Work 4 rows of C, 2 rows of D, then 4 rows of C for 2 ridges C, 1 ridge D, 2 ridges C.

Band 12: Work 4 rows of A, 2 rows of B, then 4 rows of A for 2 ridges A, 1 ridge B, 2 ridges A.

Band 13: Work 4 rows of B, 2 rows of D, then 4 rows of B for 2 ridges B, 1 ridge D, 2 ridges B.

Repeat Bands 1 through 13 for pattern. Each band = 10 rows or 5 ridges.

Note: Instead of cutting off each color and rejoining later, carry colors not in use loosely along side edges unless color will not be used for a while [more than 10 rows or so]. Vest is started at one corner and worked from the bottom up, on a 45-degree bias to vertical.

Back

Cast on 3 stitches in color D—this counts as Row 1, *mark this as Right Side.*

Row 2 [Wrong Side]—knit 1 row.

Attach a new color C. Work in Garter stitch and begin color pattern, increasing 1 stitch at the beginning and end of each Right Side row.

Continue to knit [there will be 2 more sts every other row] until 82 (84, 84) rows total or 41 (42, 42) ridges have been completed—there are 83 (85, 85) sts.

Shape one armhole:

Keeping to pattern, continue to increase at beginning of Right Side rows [right-hand side] but do not increase at end of Right Side rows [left-hand side].

When there are 104 (106, 110) rows total or 52 (53, 55) ridges, begin increasing again 1 stitch at the end of each Right Side row as well as at the beginning.

Work until there are 122 (126, 132) rows total or 61 (63, 66) ridges have been completed—there are 112 (116, 120) sts.

Shape other side:

Begin to *decrease* instead of increase 1 stitch at the beginning of each Right Side row [right-hand side] but continue to increase at the end of each Right Side row [left-hand side]. Stitch count will remain the same for this portion.

Work until there are 154 (158, 168) rows total or 77 (79, 84) ridges have been completed—there are still 112 (116, 120) sts.

Shape one shoulder:

Begin to *decrease* instead of increase 1 stitch at the end of each Right Side row [left-hand side] 13 (14, 12) times total and continue to decrease at the beginning of each Right Side row [right-hand side] as well.

When there are 179 (185, 191) rows total but only 89 (92, 95) ridges, you will have completed a Right Side row—there are 86 (88, 96) sts.

Shape back neck:

Next row [Wrong Side row]—bind off 5 (6, 7) sts at the beginning of the row—there are 81 (82, 89) sts.

Continue to decrease at the beginning and end of Right Side rows until row 202 (210, 218) has been completed for 101 (105, 109) ridges—there are 60 (59, 63) sts.

Shape other armhole:

Next row [Right Side row]—bind off 12 (12, 14) sts at the beginning of the row, decrease at the end of the row—there are 47 (46, 49) sts after the completion of the row.

Continue to decrease at the beginning and end of Right Side rows until row 218 (220, 234) has been completed for 109 (110, 117) ridges—there are 33 (38, 35) sts.

Continue to shape back neck:

Continue to decrease at the beginning of Right Side rows [right-hand side] and do not increase at end of Right Side rows [left-hand side] until 226 (230, 246) rows total have been completed for 113 (115, 123) ridges—there are 29 (33, 29) sts.

Complete other shoulder:

Continue to decrease at the beginning and end of Right Side rows.

When there are 251 (259, 271) rows total but only 125 (129, 135) ridges, you will have completed a Right Side row—3 sts remain.

Bind off remaining 3 sts on next Wrong Side row.

Front

Work same as for back, up through "Shape one shoulder" steps.

Shape front neck:

Next row [Wrong Side row]—bind off 23 (22, 27) sts at the beginning of the row—there are 63 (66, 69) sts.

Keeping to pattern, continue to decrease at beginning of Right Side rows [right-hand side] but do not increase at end of Right Side rows [left-hand side].

When 202 (210, 218) rows have been completed for 101 (105, 109) ridges—there are 52 (54, 56) sts.

■

Work other armhole shaping by binding off 12 (12, 14) sts at the beginning of the row—there are 40 (42, 42) sts after the completion of the row.

Continue to decrease at the beginning of Right Side rows [right-hand side] but do not increase at end of Right Side rows [left-hand side].

When 226 (230, 246) rows total have been completed for 113 (115, 123) ridges—there are 29 (33, 29) sts.

■

Complete other shoulder as for back.

Finishing

Sew side and shoulder seams. Using color D and double-pointed needles (dpn), with Right Side facing you, work I-cord edging along all edges [armholes, neck, and bottom] as follows:

With dpn, cast on 3 sts, then pick up and knit 1 st, with Right Side facing you, from edge you want trimmed—there are now 4 sts on dpn. Slide sts back to the beginning of dpn. With another dpn and Right Side still facing you, ★k 2, k next 2 sts together through the *back* loops, pick up another st from edge, slide sts back to the beginning of dpn. Repeat from ★ until desired length. Note the spacing of the picked-up sts and make sure that cord is neither too snug nor too loose. Sew end to beginning of cord when complete.

Buttonless Evening Cardi-Jacket
| Cher Underwood

CITY: Chicago, IL
AGE: 28

Lily M. Chin

Cher's motto in knitting (as in life) seems to be "the more complicated, the better!" She is totally devoted to anything involving cables, interesting textures, and complex shaping. Having been a knitter since the age of twelve, when her mom got her one of those Coats & Clark learn-to books, a pair of needles, and some yarn, she gets a charge out of challenging herself with more intricate projects.

Away from her needles, Cher works in the graphics department of an investment bank (where her boss is very cool about her using occasional downtime to knit!) as well as doing the odd bit of acting on stage and on camera. She's done some children's theater recently, as well as industrial film work. Her other interests include playing guitar, web design, and voice lessons ("I'm going to get my high E back if it kills me!").

Cher says, "I suppose my knitting is like anything else I do: usually for fun, sometimes for money, and always with love."

Inspiration

Cher enjoys working with double-knitting-weight yarn with an average gauge of 5.5 stitches per inch. Lighter yarn means less bulk and more refinement and drape. She also wanted to make something that would be pleasant next to the skin.

She thought in terms of evening wear, as she likes her fancy clothes still to be comfortable. Since we were partial to the idea of a fun, sparkly yarn for evening, we opted for a dressy cardigan with minimal shaping. The interest will come more from an intriguing yarn choice.

From a practical point of view, when going out to bars or dancing, a girl freezes in the car or cab and restaurant, and needs a second layer. Then, inside the bar or club, it is about a billion degrees. This dressy cardigan can be slipped on and off easily and it looks fab. I suggested a buttonless front-opening. This meant not having to deal with buttonholes and buttonbands. I've heard stories from even seasoned knitters who just cannot get over this hurdle and they go buttonless as a result (I have seen this even on people at knitting conventions). Cher was more than amenable as she doesn't really enjoy the buttonhole/band process herself. A strategically placed brooch would do just fine for those who need to feel more secure.

As far as colors go, Cher loves jewel tones—burgundies, purples, plums, deep greens, bluish reds (not orangey ones), as well as navy—basically, any of the colors that fit into the "winter" palette. Of course, for the hip, urbane individual Cher is known to be, black and white are *de rigueur* in the wardrobe.

I chose a mohair with metallic glints, but Cher was initially concerned about whether it would pass the "bra test." This is when you place some of the yarn into the brassiere to see if it itches or scratches—the yarn passed this bra test. Cher was pleased with the name of the yarn as well: "I have an aunt Odessa a generation or two back, so it tickled me to hear the name."

Cher wanted the boxy cardigan to be hip-length. As she puts it, "This seems to visually lessen the bubble butt." I gave her 6 inches of ease to achieve this effect, as the knit fabric was light and slightly drapey. We aimed for an almost loose tension to bring out the fuzz texture. When we got a swatch we were happy with, I took Cher's measurements, did the math, worked out the shaping, and gave her a set of directions to follow.

A nice, square armhole is in keeping with the classic look of this jacket. Besides being incredibly easy to do, it has straight lines we liked. Yet because of the yarn and fabric, there's a diaphanous feel to the sweater; it's sort of like being wrapped in a soft mohair cloud of style.

Although three-quarter-length sleeves are in, Cher's generally not a fan of them because of what she calls her "monkey arms." She envisioned slightly long sleeves. After all, dashing in and out of those holiday soirées can be awfully chilly!

We liked wide Garter stitch bands on the front, knitted at the same time as the sweater. A concern was that Garter stitch has a shorter row gauge than the Stockinette stitch sitting next door. However, with this particular yarn, which is not very elastic, the Garter stitch band wound up not pulling up much at all. Steam blocking afterward straightened out any discrepancies in length.

I wanted the body beneath the underarms worked in one piece on a long circular needle. Fewer seams appeal to many knitters. Cher concurred, saying, "This should also give it more of that flowy, drapey, diaphanous look I was aiming at."

Although the shape of the cardigan is boxy and straight, I think it's important in an evening sweater to make it simple yet *refined*. Sloped shoulders impart a much better look and fit, as does shaping for the back neck. It's a little more effort, but everything else remains pretty easy.

At first, Cher was confused that the Garter stitch bottom band called for smaller needles. This is because Garter stitch spreads laterally and is slightly wider than the Stockinette over it. Begin with smaller needles to keep the edges from flaring. Just don't forget to change the needle size after completing the border.

The collar is the final touch that lends a more finished and elegant look. Garter stitch is reversible, so the collar can be worn up or down for warmth or style. It is both functional and decorative.

Standard/relaxed fit with square sleeves

Finished Size: Garment measures 40 (44, 48)" at bust and is 22.5 (23, 23.5)" long.

Finished Measurements:

- **A.** Back Bottom = 20 (22, 24)"
- **B.** Across shoulders = 16 (17, 18)"
- **C.** Each shoulder width = 5"
- **D.** Neck width = 6 (7, 8)"
- **E.** Body length = 13.5"
- **F.** Armhole length = 8 (8.5, 9)"
- **G.** Shoulder slope = 1"
- **H.** Half front width = 10 (11, 12)"
- **I.** Borders = 2"
- **J.** Front neck depth = 2.5"
- **K.** Sleeve width at bottom = 8.5 (9, 9.5)"
- **L.** Sleeve width at top = 16 (17, 18)"
- **M.** Sleeve length to underarm = 18"
- **N.** Sleeve "cap" = 2 (2.5, 3)"

Materials:

- Jaeger/Westminster "Odessa" (65% mohair, 31% acrylic, 4% polyester metal, 50g, appx 209yd/190m): 6 (6, 7) skeins #166 Ruby.
- 24" circular knitting needles in sizes 7, or whatever size it takes to get the gauge, and one size smaller.
- Stitch markers.
- Stitch holders.

Gauge: 17 sts and 28 rows = 4" in Stockinette st on larger needles after steam blocking.

Special Notes: The body fronts and back are worked all in one wide piece, then separated at the armholes. Use the circular needles as if they were separate straight needles and work all parts back and forth to produce flat pieces.

Slip-slip-knit is described on page 25.

Body

With needles one size smaller than that used for swatch, cast on 172 (188, 204) sts. Work Garter st [k every row] for 2" for bottom border.

Next row (designate as Right Side)—switch to larger needles that were used for swatch, k 9 for center front border, place a st marker onto the needle, k 154 (170, 186), place a st marker onto the needle, k last 9 sts for other center front border. From here on, just slip the st markers as you work [they're there to keep your place].

Keep first and last 9 center front border sts in Garter st [k every row] and the center 154 (170, 186) sts in Stockinette st [p the Wrong Side rows and k the Right Side rows] and work until piece measures 13.5" total; end by finishing a Wrong Side row.

Separate for armholes:

Next row or the Right Side—k 35 (37, 39), ★bind off the next 16 (20, 24) sts for underarm★, k until there are 70 (74, 78) sts after the bind-off; repeat from ★ to ★, k remainder of sts. There are 35 (37, 39) sts for each of the fronts and 70 (74, 78) sts for the back.

Place the sts of both fronts onto st holders. With Wrong Side facing you, join a ball of yarn to the back.

Back

Begin with a Wrong Side row and work in Stockinette st over these 70 (74, 78) sts until armholes measure 8 (8.5, 9)"; end ready to work a Right Side row.

Shape shoulders and back neck:

Bind off 4 sts at the beginning of the next row, k across—66 (70, 74) sts.

Next row, a Wrong Side row—bind off 4 sts at the beginning of the row, p another 22 sts (there are 23 sts on the right needle, including the st left by the last bound-off st), bind off the next center 16 (20, 24) sts, p the other shoulder to the end.

There are 23 sts for each shoulder. You will be working both sides of these shoulders at the same time but separately, each with its own individual ball of yarn.

Next row, a Right Side row—bind off 4 sts at the beginning of the row, k to the end of this shoulder, join another ball of yarn to the other side with the Right Side still facing you and bind off the first 3 sts, k the other shoulder to the end.

Next row, a Wrong Side row—bind off 4 sts at the beginning of the row, p to the end of this shoulder, bind off the first 3 sts at the beginning of the other shoulder, p the other shoulder to the end.

There are 16 sts at each shoulder.

Repeat the last 2 rows (no need to join another

ball, though, it's already been joined) and bind off the 4 sts at the shoulders' outer edges as usual, but bind off only 2 sts at the neck edges. There are 10 sts at each shoulder.

Next row, a Right Side row—bind off 4 sts at the beginning of the row, k to within the last 3 sts at the end of this shoulder, k 2 together to decrease, begin the other shoulder with a k 1, slip-slip-knit decrease, then k to the end. Work a p row and bind off 5 sts at the beginning of the first shoulder, p across other shoulder. There are 5 sts at each shoulder.

Bind off all sts in k on the next Right Side row. You can end off the yarns, leaving about 12" to sew up the shoulders together later.

Left Front

Slip the 35 (37, 39) sts of the left front onto the needles with Wrong Side facing you. Keeping the Stockinette sts in Stockinette and the center front borders in Garter st, work until armhole measures 6.5 (7, 7.5)" (measure the Stockinette portion for height). End ready to work a Wrong Side row.

Shape front neck:

Bind off 9 (9, 10) sts at the beginning of the next Wrong Side row—26 (28, 29) sts remain.

Next row or the Right Side [a Decrease row]—k to within the last 4 sts, slip-slip-knit the next 2 sts together to decrease, k the last 2 sts—25 (27, 28) sts remain.

Next row or the Wrong Side—p across.

Size Small: ★Work 2 rows in Stockinette st, [work Decrease row and Wrong Side row] twice; repeat from ★ once more.

Size Medium and Large: Repeat the last 2 rows (6, 7) times.

At the same time, when the piece measures 8 (8.5, 9)" from the beginning of the armhole shaping, end with a Wrong Side row.

Next row or the Right Side—continue to shape the front neck but bind off the first 4 sts at the beginning of the row. Bind off 4 sts at the beginning of the Right Side rows another 3 times. Bind off the remaining 5 sts on the last Right Side row.

Right Front

Slip the 35 (37, 39) sts of the left front onto the needles with Wrong Side facing you. Keeping the Stockinette sts in Stockinette and the center front borders in Garter st, work until armhole measures 6.5 (7, 7.5)" (measure the Stockinette portion for height). End ready to work a Right Side row.

Shape front neck:

Bind off 9 (9, 10) sts at the beginning of the next Right Side row—26 (28, 29) sts remain.

Next row or the Wrong Side—p across.

Next row or the Right Side—k 2, k the next 2 sts together, k to the end—25 (27, 28) sts remain.

Next row or the Wrong Side—p across.

Size Small: ★Work 2 rows in Stockinette st, [work Decrease row and Wrong Side row] twice; repeat from ★ once more.

Size Medium and Large: Repeat the last 2 rows (6, 7) times.

At the same time, when the piece measures 8 (8.5, 9)" from the beginning of the armhole shaping, end with a Right Side row.

Next row or the Wrong Side—continue to shape the front neck but bind off the first 4 sts at the beginning of the row. Bind off 4 sts at the beginning of the Wrong Side rows another 3 more times. Bind off the remaining 5 sts on the last Right Side row.

Sleeves

With needles one size smaller than that used for swatch, cast on 38 (40, 42) sts. Work Garter st (k every row) for 2" for bottom border.

Next row (designate as Right Side)—switch to larger needles that were used for swatch and begin Stockinette st. At the same time, increase fully fashioned [after first 2 sts and before the last 2 sts] every 6th row 12 (15, 17) times, then every 8th row 4 (2, 0) times. Work even on 70 (74, 78) sts until piece measures 18" total from the beginning. Mark either end of last row. Work another 2 (2.5, 3)" straight for a total of 20 (20.5, 21)". Bind off loosely.

Finishing

Block pieces to measurements. Sew shoulder seams. Set in sleeves by sewing tops of sleeves to straight part of armholes, then sew straight portion at tops of sleeves (above markers) to bound-off armhole sts. Sew sleeve seams.

Collar:

With Right Side facing you and using smaller needles, begin at right front neck. Pick up and k 19 (21, 23) sts evenly spaced around right front neck, 26 (30, 34) sts across back neck and another 19 (21, 23) evenly spaced around left front neck—64 (72, 80) sts total.

Begin Garter st, work until collar measures 3.5", ending with a Wrong Side row. Bind off loosely using larger needles.

Lily M. Chin

ꙮ A Trio of Pillows:

Chenille Pillow, Slip-Stitch Pillow, and Aran Pillow

| Katherine Meyers

CITY: Dallas, TX

AGE: 27

Though originally from North Carolina, Katherine now lives about five minutes from downtown Dallas. A graduate of the University of North Carolina at Chapel Hill in 1996, she is working on her Ph.D. in biochemistry and molecular biology at the University of Texas Southwestern Medical Center in Dallas. After she finishes many years of apprenticeship research, she looks forward to one day having a lab of her own and doing research as a professor at a university. Her scientific interests lie in the realm of gene expression and regulation, which has applications both in understanding cancer and in gene therapy.

Her mother taught her to knit and crochet when Katherine was in middle school. By the time Katherine was in high school, she was completely hooked on knitting. Maybe it took a little longer for her to really "get it" since she's left-handed (though she was taught to knit right-handed). Though she's happy with this circumstance, she doesn't have a problem teaching herself new techniques and reading instructions.

She's taught several friends to knit, and loves doing so, as it helps add to the population that breaks the stereotypes of knitters. She's a big fan of textures and cables and she can usually be found designing or working on a project that involves them both. The challenges in designing and knitting are what make them so attractive to her. Katherine considers herself a good knitter; she's never really found a problem she can't find some solution to. She always has several projects going on at once, though. That way, when she gets stuck on one, she can take a break and make some progress on another one. Katherine also enjoys going to the symphony and art museums in the area, reading, and getting outdoors.

Inspiration

Katherine's definitely into cables and textured stitches without lots of colorwork. However, what she had in mind was to do decorator pillows—the types you find at Pier 1 or Pottery Barn. These would work well for a simple, beginner's project. And of course, pillows are great for giving a new look to hand-me-down furniture or plain futons.

Pillows provide a good opportunity to try out a few knitting techniques without taking on a dauntingly large commitment, so I suggested that Katherine do pillows using some colorwork as well. To get variety, I said, why not one textured, one colored, and one relatively plain in fancy yarn?

As a compromise, we opted to do slip-stitch "mosaic" knitting for colorwork. I had just the right pattern in mind, one that I'd come up with

a few years ago for a yarn company. I call it Turkish Tiles, and Katherine really loved the effect. The complex look belies its ease of execution. The sturdy and affordable yarns we used come in quite a nice variety of colors, and the worsted-weight wool blend is definitely meant for colorwork.

At first, Katherine had doubts about the fancy chenille yarn. She really likes chenille, but feared "worming." Chenille has a tendency to pull away from the fabric and form pop-out loops. I reassured her that this would not happen as I've used this yarn a lot in the past. I've learned that knitting chenille in a firmer tension alleviates worming.

The knit-purl combination Katherine came up with for the chenille is especially elegant. Despite being worked in a highly textured yarn in a dark color, the stitch pattern shows up beautifully and looks so velvety and plush.

For the cabled project, Katherine was looking forward to working with the worsted-weight blend of alpaca/wool/acrylic. She came up with a wonderful combination of cables. They are placed in a mirror-image arrangement so that the patterns are easy to remember, and the cables themselves are easy row repeats. I love how complicated the patterns seem, yet they are pretty effortless.

Fun and quick, decorative and functional,

these pillows make great gifts too. I'm sure many will be made with your own variations in color or size or stitch or arrangement. Looking back, the only thing I might have added to these lush, plump poufs would be tassels at the corners. This is definitely an option.

Instructions | Chenille Pillow

Finished Size: 16" × 16"

Materials:
- Lion Brand "Chenille Thick-n-Quick" (91% acrylic, 9% rayon, 6oz, appx 199yds): 3 skeins # 147 Purple.
- Size 10 knitting needles or size needed to obtain gauge.
- 16" pillow form.

Gauge: 8 sts and 12 rows = 4" in k 2, p 2 pattern.

Pillow Top (Make 2)

Cast on 32 stitches.

Row 1—[k 2, p 2] 8 times.

Row 2—repeat Row 1.

Row 3—[p 2, k 2] 8 times.

Row 4—repeat Row 3.

Repeat Rows 1 through 4 until piece measures 16". Bind off loosely.

Finishing

Sew together pieces, leaving one edge open. Insert pillow form. Complete sewing of last open edge.

Instructions | Slip-Stitch Pillow

Finished Size: 14" × 14"

Materials:
- Lion Brand "Wool-Ease" (80% acrylic, 20% wool, 2 oz, appx 197yds): 1 skein each #153 Black (color A), #189 Butterscotch (color B), and #138 Cranberry (color C).
- Sizes 7 and 8 knitting needles, or sizes needed to obtain gauge.
- 14" pillow form.

Gauge: 18 st and 32 rows = 4" in slip-stitch pattern on smaller needles.

Special Note: Larger needles are used for the first and last 2 rows to prevent excessive tightness along the edges since the pattern will condense the fabric. Instead of cutting off each color and rejoining later, carry colors not in use loosely along side edges. Always slip sts as if to purl. Pattern stitch is a multiple of 10 sts plus 1 extra.

Pillow Top (Make 2)

With larger needles and color A cast on 61 sts.

Row 1 [Right Side]—knit across.

Row 2 [Wrong Side]—change to smaller needles, purl across.

Row 3—with color B, k 3, ★[slip 1 with yarn in back, k 1] 2 times, slip 1 with yarn in back, k 5; repeat from ★ across, ending with k 3.

Row 4—k 3, ★ [slip 1 with yarn in front, k 1] 2 times, slip 1 with yarn in front, k 5★; repeat from ★ across, ending with k 3.

Row 5—p 3 ★ [slip 1 with yarn in back, p 1] 2 times, slip 1 with yarn in back, p 5; repeat from ★ across, ending with p 3.

Row 6—repeat Row 4.

Row 7—repeat Row 5.

Row 8—repeat Row 4.

Row 9—change to color A, k across.

Row 10—p across.

Row 11—with color C, k 10, ★slip 1 with yarn in back, k 9; repeat from ★ across, ending with an extra k 1.

Row 12—p 10, ★slip 1 with yarn in front, p 9; repeat from ★ across, ending with an extra p 1.

Row 13—repeat Row 11.

Row 14—repeat Row 12.

Row 15—repeat Row 11.

Row 16—repeat Row 12.

Row 17—change to color A, k across.

Row 18—p across.

Repeat Rows 3 through 18 until piece measures 14". End on Row 8, then work Rows 9 and 10 with larger needles. Bind off loosely.

Finishing

Block pieces and sew together, leaving one edge open. Insert pillow form. Complete sewing of last open edge.

Instructions | Aran Pillow

Finished Size: 18" × 18"

Materials:

- Lion Brand "Al-Pa-Ka" (30% alpaca, 30 % wool, 40% acrylic, 50gm/1.75oz, appx 107yds): 6 skeins #149 Silver Gray.
- Size 6 knitting needles, or size needed to obtain gauge.
- Cable needle.
- 18" pillow form.

Gauge: 18 st and 25 rows = 4" in Stockinette stitch.

Cable abbreviations:

CF4 (Cable Front 4): Slip 2 stitches to cable needle, hold in front, knit 2, knit 2 stitches from cable needle.

CB4 (Cable Back 4): Slip 2 stitches to cable needle, hold in back, knit 2, knit 2 stitches from cable needle.

Special Note: Pattern is an 8-row repeat using only basic 4-stitch cables.

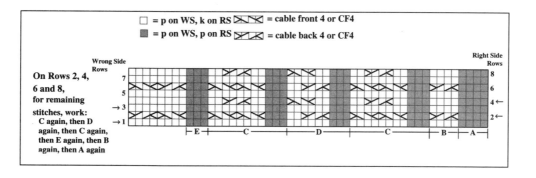

□ = p on WS, k on RS ⊠⊠ = cable front 4 or CF4
■ = p on WS, p on RS ⊠⊠ = cable back 4 or CF4

On Rows 2, 4, 6 and 8, for remaining stitches, work: C again, then D again, then C again, then E again, then B again, then A again

Pillow Top (Make 2)

Cast on 92 stitches.

Row 1 [Wrong Side] establish pattern—k 4, p 4, k 3, p 8, k 3, p 6, (k 3, p 8) 3 times, k 3, p 6, k 3, p 8, k 3, p 4, k 4.

Row 2 [Right Side]—p 4, CB4, p 3, (CF4) 2 times, p 3, (CB4, k 2), p 3, (CF4) 2 times, p 3, CF4, CB4, p 3, (CF4) 2 times, p 3, (CB4, k 2), p 3, (CF4) 2 times, p 3, CB4, p 4.

Rows 3, 5, 7, and 9 or all odd-numbered or Wrong Side rows—repeat Row 1. Basically, k the k sts and p the p sts as they present themselves.

Row 4—p 4, k 4, p 3, (k 2, CB4, k 2), p 3, (k 2, CF4), p 3, (k 2, CB4, k 2), p 3, k 8, p 3, (k 2, CB4, k 2), p 3, (k 2, CF4), p 3, (k 2, CB4, k 2), p 3, k 4, p 4.

Row 6—p 4, CB4, p 3, (CF4) 2 times, p 3, (CB4, k 2), p 3, (CF4) 2 times, p 3, CB4, CF4, p 3, (CF4) 2 times, p 3, (CB4, k 2), p 3, (CF4) 2 times, p 3, CB4, p 4.

Row 8—p 4, k 4, p 3, (k 2, CB4, k 2), p 3, (k 2, CF4), p 3, (k 2, CB4, k 2), p 3, k 8, p 3, (k 2, CB4, k 2), p 3, (k 2, CF4), p 3, (k 2, CB4, k 2), p 3, k 4, p 4.

Row 9—repeat Row 1.

Repeat Rows 2 through 9 for pattern until piece measures 18". End ready to work a Wrong Side row. Bind off loosely.

Finishing

Block pieces and sew together, leaving one edge open. Insert pillow form. Complete sewing of last open edge.

Sleeveless Tank Top/Vest | Cheryl Kellman

CITY: New York, NY
AGE: 38

Lily M. Chin

Knitting is Cheryl's passion. It is a very important part of her life, though she came to it in a circuitous manner.

Cheryl lives in New York City, which is, according to her, one of the greatest cities on earth. She shares her house with her cat, Gregia, who is the spunkiest brat on the planet, again according to Cheryl. N.Y.C. is a very diverse amalgamation of many cultures, tastes, and fashions, Cheryl explains, and she is always bombarded visually with all kinds of stimulation, which help her to develop her creative side.

Cheryl happens to be tall, slim, and leggy so fashion comes naturally to her. But she's particular when it comes to clothes and wants outfits that fit her just the right way. She started with sewing but found it too unforgiving if you cut the fabric wrong. So she went to machine knitting and hand knitting, which she continues to do to this day.

She docs some knitting for pay (samples for designers and yarn stores) and some for fun. She knits every day but does not knit for a living. Her "real job" is on Wall Street in investment banking. She works for a brokerage firm in its technology department, which she finds stimulating, challenging, and stressful. She uses knitting to relax after a tough day at work. The more stress she feels on the job, the more prolific she is with her knitting. (I always wondered why she has so many sweaters!)

Cheryl says, "I love the feel of fibers through my hands, the creative process of making lovely garments, and the pleasure of the complete work. Wall Street pays the bills but knitting is my passion."

Inspiration

Cheryl also writes, "When Lily asked me to participate in this book project I jumped at the chance! I loved the opportunity to work with the talented Ms. Lily to create a beautiful wearable garment for the beginning knitter." I hope we have achieved that result with this interesting top for both day wear (under suits) and evening wear (over a long skirt).

Cheryl loves shapely clothing. Luckily, she has the figure for it. We agreed on deeply cut armholes to create almost a halter look to this tank top. This is not only fashionable, it highlights the bust and shows off toned upper arms. To add more detail, a funnel neck was in order. More substance at the neck stabilizes a somewhat skimpy garment. Just be sure to bind off stitches loosely or the sweater will not fit over your head. Use needles one or two sizes larger to do this if necessary. The waist begins small and stitches are increased at the sides to fill out for the bust. Even if you're not so fortunate as to be well endowed,

this shaping will create the illusion of an hourglass figure.

A highly textured, small allover-stitch of knit-purl combinations added lots of visual appeal yet kept things pretty easy to follow. This is nothing but a rib variation. When working more involved shapings into a garment, keeping the stitch simple is advantageous. It allows you to concentrate more on the increases and decreases taking place.

Since the basis for this stitch is, by and large, Reverse Stockinette, I feature Stockinette at the edges for less eyestrain when seaming. I almost always use mattress seaming, as I think this is the most invisible and the most elegant. The use of two Stockinette stitches at the edges make it very clear where to insert the sewing needle. It also leaves a beautiful decorative "frame" around the seams. Furthermore, picking up stitches for trims is easier.

The increasing and decreasing occur within these selvedge stitches, thus leaving the selvedges unfettered, free and clear for seaming or picking up. Also, I'm quite particular about the types of decreasing that go on. Mirror-image decreases (knit 2 together along one edge but slip-slip-knit along the other) create symmetry and balance. It is this kind of attention to detail that sets apart an okay sweater from a well-crafted, knock-out sweater. It is this type of workmanship that garners higher prices in the retail, ready-to-wear world.

Of course, materials are also important in a stand-out garment. This luscious blend of mohair and wool is more than affordable for the quality, especially considering the piece is not all that large.

We loosened the gauge slightly. That is, we knitted it at a slightly looser tension than what the yarn might normally call for. This infuses more drape into a garment and is particularly important in a closer-fitting piece such as this. However, it is not so loose as to be see-through.

As Cheryl said, a piece like this means wardrobe versatility. It can be conservative and demure under a jacket or cardigan. It can also serve as a vest of sorts over a tight, long-sleeved T-shirt. It is most sexy and suggestive when worn alone.

Instructions | Sleeveless Tank Top/Vest

Shaped and close-fitting

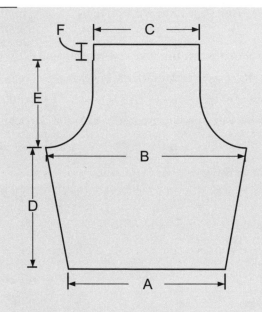

Finished Size: Garment measures 31 (33, 35, 37, 39)" at chest and is 17.5 (18, 18.5, 19, 19.5)" long without collar.

Finished Measurements:

A. Back/front bottom waist = 11.5 (12.5, 13.5, 14.5, 15.5)"

B. Back/front bust = 15.5 (16.5, 17.5, 18.5, 19.5)"

C. Neck width = 9 (9.5, 9.5, 9.5, 10)"

D. Body length = 11.25"

E. Armhole length = 6.25 (6.75, 7.25, 7.75, 8.25)"

F. Collar depth = 3"

Materials:

- Bryspun "Kid-N-Ewe" (50% wool, 50% mohair, 50g appx 120yds): 4 (4, 4, 4, 5) skeins #490 Teal.
- Knitting needles and 16" circular needles in size 7 or whatever size it takes to get the gauge.
- Stitch markers.
- Stitch holders.

Gauge: 18 sts and 27 rows = 4" in Beaded Rib st after washing and steam blocking.

Special Notes: Selvedge stitches in Stockinette [k Right Side rows, p Wrong Side rows] are used at the beginning and end of every row. The use of these selvedge or edge stitches ensures very neat seaming and are decorative as well. St markers help distinguish these selvedges from rest of knitting in Beaded Rib st pattern. Slip st markers as you work.

Slip-slip-knit = [slip next st as if to knit] twice, insert the left-hand needle from left to right through the fronts of these 2 sts, then knit the two together in this position [through their back loops].

Beaded Rib Stitch Pattern

Pattern is a 2-st repeat worked over an odd number of sts.

Row 1, a Wrong Side row—k across.

Row 2, a Right Side row—★p 1, k 1; repeat from ★ across, end with p 1. Repeat Rows 1 and 2 for Beaded Rib pattern.

Front or Back (Make 2 Alike)

Cast on 53 (59, 63, 67, 73) sts.

Row 1, a Wrong Side row—p 2 as selvedges, place st marker onto needle, begin Beaded Rib pattern, work to within last 2 sts, place st marker onto needle, p last 2 sts as selvedges.

Next row, a Right Side row—k 2 as selvedges, continue Beaded Rib pattern between the st markers, end k 2 as selvedges.

Repeat last 2 rows until there are a total of 6 rows, end by finishing a Right Side row.

Shape for bust:

Next row or the Wrong Side—p 2 selvedge sts, increase in next st, work to within 1 st of last marker, increase in next st, p last 2 selvedge sts—55 (61, 65, 69, 75) sts.

Continue to increase in this manner every 6th row 3 more times, then every 8th row 5 times, incorporating the increased-sts into the established Beaded Rib pattern. There are 2 more sts with each increase row.

Work even on 71 (77, 81, 85, 91) sts until piece measures 11.25" total from beginning, end ready to work a Wrong Side row.

Shape for armholes:

Keeping to pattern and removing previous st markers, bind off 4 (4, 5, 5, 6) sts at the beginning of the next 2 rows, then bind off 2 sts at the beginning of the next 2 rows—59 (65, 67, 71, 75) sts.

Next row, [a Decrease row], worked on Wrong Side—p 2 for selvedges, place st marker onto needle, k 2 together to decrease, work to within last 4 sts, slip-slip-knit to decrease, place st marker onto needle, p last 2 sts for selvedges—57 (63, 65, 69, 73) sts.

Next row, a Right Side row—k 2 for selvedges, keep to established Beaded Rib pattern to next st marker, k last 2 sts for selvedges.

Repeat last 2 rows 4 (6, 7, 7, 8) more times—49 (51, 51, 55, 57) sts. Work 2 rows on 49 (51, 51, 55, 57) sts in established pattern, then repeat Decrease row on next Wrong Side row—47 (49, 49, 53, 55) sts.

★Work 3 rows in established pattern, then repeat Decrease row on next Wrong Side row—45 (47, 47, 51, 53) sts. Repeat from ★ 0 (0, 0, 2, 2) more times having 45 (47, 47, 49, 51) sts after first repeat and 45 (47, 47, 47, 49) sts after second repeat.

Work even in established pattern on 45 (47,

47, 49) sts until armholes measure 6.25 (6.75, 7.25, 7.75, 8.25)" total from the beginning of armhole shaping, end ready to work a Right Side row.

Shape for shoulders:

Keeping to established patterns, bind off 2 sts at the beginning of the next 2 rows—41 (43, 43, 43, 45) sts. Place sts onto st holder to be worked later.

Finishing

Block pieces to measurements. Sew shoulder seams.

Collar:

With Wrong Side facing you and using 16" circular needles, knit across all 41 (43, 43, 43, 45) sts on st holder of one piece, pick up 1 st at shoul-der seam, knit across all 41 (43, 43, 43, 45) sts on st holder of other piece, pick up 1 st at shoulder seam, place st marker onto needle to mark beginning/end of rounds—84 (88, 88, 88, 92) sts. From here on, work in the round with Wrong Side of piece facing you at all times.

Round 1—[k 1, p 1] *or* [p 1, k 1] all around to keep to pattern.

Round 2—k around.

Repeat Rounds 1 and 2 until collar measures about 3" high, end with a Round 1, bind off loosely in k.

Armhole trim:

Sew side seams. With Right Side facing you and using 16" circular needles, begin at underarm and pick up and k sts evenly around. Bind off loosely in knit. Repeat for other armhole.

J.A.B. Photography

Bulky, Boxy, Seamless Pullover

| Lisa Sewell

CITY: Salt Lake City, UT
AGE: 39

Lisa was born and reared in Salt Lake City. She grew up Catholic there, and says, "Where I come from, you always need to spell this out." She completed her B.A. degree in political science and communications at Linfield College, a small liberal arts college in McMinnville, Oregon. She then went back to Salt Lake City, married, biked around the country for eight months, settled in Durango, Colorado, moved back to Salt Lake City, got divorced, and started being single again in her thirties. She has three cats: Tenpenny, Buddy, and Meers.

Lisa did some bike racing and got into triathlons in 1994. She started a tri-club in Utah called the Desert Sharks. She hopes to do her first Ironman competition in Canada in August 2001, when she is forty. Lisa has worked in the nonprofit world her entire adult life—first in public radio and now at the Utah Arts Festival, where she is the assistant director.

Lisa tends to be a type-A personality who can't handle being idle. Hence, she suffers from "knitting-in-the-car syndrome." She doesn't knit while she drives, her project just sits on her lap and when she gets to a stoplight, or if she's stuck in traffic, she picks it up and knits! It's usually mindless or "auto-pilot" knitting, but she pretty much completed her boxy red pullover while "car knitting." She personally thinks there would be a lot less road rage if more drivers would knit!

As for her knitting life, she started a bit in college when she was in a play that required the character to knit. Once she graduated, she was hanging out at her parents' home one day, when she picked up an old book of her mother's and thought, "Hmm, I wonder if I can do this . . ." and away she went.

She started teaching for proprietor Nancy Bush at the Wooly West yarn shop in late 1988 or '89. She currently teaches for proprietor Vonnie Wildfoerster at the Black Sheep Wool Company. Lisa teaches beginning knitting, Fair Isle (her favorite type of knitting), Finishing, Mittens, Latvian Mittens, and Norwegian knitting. She's unique among her knitting friends in that she only does one project at a time (maybe two, if you count the car project) and she doesn't have a yarn stash! Well, she does have Shetland and Satakieli yarn.

Her favorite needle size is 2. She has a group of women who have been meeting to knit every Wednesday night for ten years now and another group that has met before work at a coffee shop on Friday mornings since 1986!

Inspiration

Lisa is partial to natural fibers. Her idea was to do a big, chunky sweater since that's what's in these days. Chunky sweaters are indeed all the rage and the yarn we chose, bulky wool with a touch of mohair—in a drop-dead lipstick red (Lisa's also partial to reds)—is actually from an American yarn producer.

A short, cropped pullover was in order. This way, the weight of the sweater, which is very thick, would not impede Lisa's active and athletic lifestyle. Keeping the sweater in Stockinette stitch not only reduces thickness in an already-bulky yarn, it is most conducive to easy knitting (Remember, she did this while driving!). The rib is not a "true" rib but a variation called Beaded Rib, where every other row is knit across rather than knit 1, purl 1. This does not pull in as much, to maintain that boxy look.

Many knitters have an aversion to sewing seams. As a result, countless sweater pieces sit a long time in closets, awaiting finishing. Here is an example of how a sweater can be made, then, without seams.

Lisa wanted to knit the sweater circularly to the underarms, then separate the back from the front and work each one back and forth between the armholes. The neck shaping would be simple, and the shoulders would be knit together as they were bound off. Sleeves would then be picked up and knit downward circularly with decreases. Thus, there would be no seams!

The 3-needle bind-off Lisa used to join the

shoulders works from "live" stitches on a front needle and a back one. It's a good method for reducing the bulkiness of sewing the shoulders together.

To do the 3-needle bind-off, begin by holding the stitches of one shoulder on one needle in front or in back of the stitches of the corresponding shoulder on another needle. With a third needle, knit 1 stitch from the front needle together with 1 stitch from the back needle (i.e., go through front-needle stitch, then through back-needle stitch, knit them both off together). Repeat with each of the next stitches but *bind off in the process* after knitting them both off together.

Instructions | Bulky, Boxy, Seamless Pullover
Loose-fitting with drop shoulders

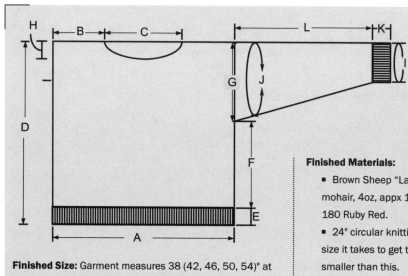

Finished Size: Garment measures 38 (42, 46, 50, 54)" at bust and is 21 (21, 21.5, 21.5, 22)" long.

Finished Measurements:

A. Back bottom = 19 (21, 23, 25, 27)"

B. Each shoulder width = 5.5 (6, 6.75, 7.75, 8.5)"

C. Neck width = 8 (9, 9.5, 9.5, 10)"

D. Body length = 21 (21, 21.5, 21.5, 22)"

E. Bottom rib depth = 3"

F. Body length above rib = 9"

G. Armhole length = 9 (9, 9.5, 9.5, 10)"

H. Front neck depth = 2.5"

I. Sleeve width at bottom = 8.5 (8.5, 9.25, 9.25 10)"

J. Sleeve width at top = 18 (18, 19, 19, 20)"

K. Sleeve rib depth = 2"

L. Sleeve length to underarm above rib = 16.5 (16, 15.5, 15, 14.5)"

M. Total sleeve length = 18.5 (18, 17.5, 17, 16.5)"

Finished Materials:

- Brown Sheep "Lamb's Pride Bulky" (85% wool, 15% mohair, 4oz, appx 125yds): 6 (6, 7, 9, 10) skeins #M-180 Ruby Red.
- 24" circular knitting needles in size 10.5, or whatever size it takes to get the gauge, and needles one size smaller than this.
- Double-pointed needles and/or 16" circular needles of these same sizes.
- Stitch markers.
- Stitch holders.

Finished Gauge: 13 sts and 20 rows = 4" in Stockinette st on larger needles after steam blocking.

Special Notes: The body is worked circularly [in the round], then separated at the armholes and worked back and forth in rows. Sleeves are also worked circularly by picking up sts around armholes and working downward toward the cuffs.

Slip-slip-knit= [slip next st as if to knit] twice, insert the left-hand needle from left to right through the fronts of these 2 sts, then knit the two together in this position [through their back loops].

Body

With one size smaller 24" circular needles than that used for swatch, cast on 124 (136, 150, 162, 176) sts. Place a st marker onto the needle to signify the beginning and end of the rounds, slipping marker as you work. Join beginning to end, being careful not to twist the work, and work Beaded Rib st as follows:

Row 1—*k 1, p 1; repeat from * around.

Row 2—k around.

Repeat Rows 1 and 2 alternately for 3" total for bottom rib.

Switch to larger 24" circular needles that were used for swatch, k all rows until piece measures 12" total.

At armholes, separate for back and front:

Begin to work back and forth in Stockinette st rows (k on Right Side rows, p on Wrong Side rows).

Back

Next row or the Right Side—k 62 (68, 75, 81, 88), place the remaining 62 (68, 75, 81, 88) sts onto a st holder for front sts to be worked later.

Turn and purl. Continue working Stockinette st over these 62 (68, 75, 81, 88) sts until piece measures 9 (9, 9.5, 9.5, 10)" from separation, end ready to work a Wrong Side row.

Next row—p 18 (19, 22, 25, 28) sts, bind off the next 26 (30, 31, 31, 32) sts, purl the remaining sts—18 (19, 22, 25, 28) sts remain for each shoulder. Place the sts of each shoulder onto stitch holders.

Front

Slip the 62 (68, 75, 81, 88) sts of the front from the st holder onto the needles. Begin with a Right Side row, join yarn and work Stockinette st as for back until piece measures 6.5 (6.5, 7, 7, 7.5)" from separation, end ready to work a Wrong Side row.

Shape front neck:

P first 25 (27, 30, 33, 36) sts, join another ball of yarn and use this to bind off next center 12 (14, 15, 15, 16) sts, p to the end—25 (27, 30, 33, 36) sts remain at each shoulder.

You will be working both shoulders at the same time but separately, each with its own individual ball of yarn.

Next row or the Right Side—k across first shoulder; at next shoulder, bind off first 2 (3, 3, 3, 3) sts, k to end.

Next row or the Wrong Side—p across first shoulder; at next shoulder, bind off first 2 (3, 3, 3, 3) sts, p to end. There are 23 (24, 27, 30, 33) sts at each shoulder.

Repeat previous 2 rows but bind off only 2 sts on each row instead of 2 (3, 3, 3, 3). There are 21 (22, 25, 28, 31) sts at each shoulder.

Next row or the Right Side—k to within the last 4 sts of first shoulder, k the next 2 together, k the last 2 sts, k the first 2 sts of next shoulder, slip-slip-knit to decrease the next 2 sts together, k to the end—20 (21, 24, 27, 30) sts remain at each shoulder.

Next row or the Wrong Side—p across each shoulder. Repeat the previous 2 rows 2 more times. Place the remaining 18 (19, 22, 25, 28) sts of each side onto a stitch holder.

Sleeves (Work Twice)

Join a front and back shoulder using the 3-needle bind-off method (see page 87) with the Wrong Sides to the outside and the Right Sides facing each other.

With Right Side facing you and using 16" circular or double-pointed needles of same size that was used for swatch, pick up and k 58 (58, 62, 62, 66) sts evenly all around the armhole opening, beginning at underarm.

Join and place a st marker to designate beginning/end of rounds.

Work Stockinette st circularly [in the round] and work decrease as follows: at beginning of round, k 1, k 2 together to decrease, k to within last 3 sts, slip-slip-knit the next 2 sts together to decrease, k the last st.

Do this:

For size 38: every 6th round 6 times, then every 5th round 9 times more.

For size 42: every 5th round 15 times total.

For size 46: every 5th round 10 times, then every 4th round 6 times more.

For size 50: every 5th round 8 times, then every 4th round 8 times more.

For size 54: every 4th round 17 times total.

Work even on remaining 28 (28, 30, 30, 32) sts until sleeve measures 16.5 (16, 15.5, 15, 14.5)" total from pick-up.

Cuffs:

Switch to smaller needles than those used for swatch. Work Beaded Rib st as for body for 2" to complete cuff, using the larger needle to bind off loosely.

Finishing

Block pieces to measurements.

Collar:

With Right Side facing you and using smaller 16" circular or double-pointed needles, begin at right shoulder. Pick up and k 28 (32, 33, 33, 34) sts evenly spaced across back neck and 40 (42, 43, 43, 44) sts evenly spaced around front neck—68 (74, 76, 76, 78) sts. Work 3" in Beaded Rib st, then use larger needle to bind off loosely.

Man's Raglan-Sleeved Pullover Tunic
| Greg Soltys

CITY: Oakland, CA
AGE: 32

Lily M. Chin

Greg has been knitting since the fall of 1997. He took to it like the proverbial duck to water and has decided to teach anyone and everyone who shows an interest. They have been all people his age or younger so far.

What started out innocently enough as a mild preoccupation has escalated into a full-blown obsession. He wanted to make a scarf for a friend for Christmas and an expert knitter/coworker taught him how to cast on, knit, purl, and cast off. It was the beginning of the end, as far as he can tell. It is Greg's goal to make the world a safer place for the man who knits and to get more interesting/fashionable patterns out there for men,

in place of the usual ill-fitting "unisex" sweaters.

Knitting has been a great creative outlet for him, since his day job as a trademark paralegal at a large law firm in San Francisco offers few creative opportunities, although colleagues do not care if he knits during department meetings. In fact, some of them have started to do it, too! Greg adds, "I basically work to be able to support my knitting." Until recently, he was the only male knitter that he knew.

Inspiration

Greg gave a lot of thought to the sweater he'd like to see. He feels there is a lack of "cool" knitwear designs for men. Something that he wanted to design for himself was a striped, ribbed pullover with a very shallow V-neck. He'd seen things like it at some of the hipper stores in San Francisco and thought it couldn't be that hard.

Based on his notions, I worked out horizontal stripes via simple changes in color in a wide, mostly purled rib. Stripes are ever-popular, especially now among the Gap generation. Playing around with them is even more fun. Add the vertical texture of ribs to the horizontal colors of stripes and you've got quite a play of both hues and surface design.

The stripes can vary but we settled for: ★6 rows A, 3 rows B, 2 rows C, 3 Rows B; repeat from ★.

You may decide to try this as well: ★6 rows A, 4 rows C, 6 rows A, 2 rows B, 2 rows C, 2 rows B; repeat from ★.

Weavers use what is known as a color wrap. For every knit row in a given color, wrap the yarn once around a ruler or narrow piece of cardboard. For many rows, wrap yarn that number of times. This way, you can quickly and easily view different color combinations and proportions.

Notice how there is a color "blending" or bleeding on the purl side as you change yarns. Some may find this irksome, others think it attractive. If you are bothered by it, work a Stockinette row (k on Right Side or p on Wrong Side) for a smooth color change, then go back to where

you want Reverse Stockinette (p on Right Side, k on Wrong Side).

We actually combined both types of color changes here. The colors closer to each other (purple and green) blend or bleed and it isn't jarring or too noticeable. However, when introducing the yellow, we opted for the smoother color change on rows 9 and 11. The colors not in use should be carried loosely up the sides of the piece as you go. I showed Greg how to twist the unused color around the color in use so that there would be no long floats on the sides.

There's a lot you can do to make this interesting yet still easy to do. Stripes and ribs are just a couple of examples.

We wanted the garment to have polish. This is not a loose and baggy sweater, though it can be Casual Friday wear. Using Stockinette stitch for the ends, or selvedges, tidies up the seams. Mattress seaming is a must—if you're not familiar with it, get a good book or video on the technique and practice. Particular decreases were employed as well. A knit-2-together decrease slants the stitches to the right and a slip-slip-knit decrease slants them left. We carefully mirrored them throughout for symmetry and elegant attention to fine detail.

What is crucial to the raglan is that the stripes are the same at the beginning of the armhole shaping. If the stripes do not match from body to sleeve, the whole garment looks awkward. Thus, if you decide to make changes in sleeve or body lengths, be sure that the stripes line up at this juncture.

Greg gave me his measurements and a gauge swatch he'd made. I used his gauge numbers to come up with the pattern. We call it the "boyfriend sweater" because many knitters will want to knit one for a boyfriend . . . or for themselves.

One signature touch I'm particularly proud of is the use of the shoulder dart. In almost all raglans, the nature of the slanting armhole creates very sloped shoulders. With guys in particular in mind (though women can wear this style too), I wanted more broad and pronounced shoulder shaping. The raglan dart at the top of the sleeve caps creates this look. It takes a wee bit more concentration in the knitting, but we love the results.

Instructions | Man's Raglan-Sleeved Pullover Tunic

Standard-fitting with shallow V-neck

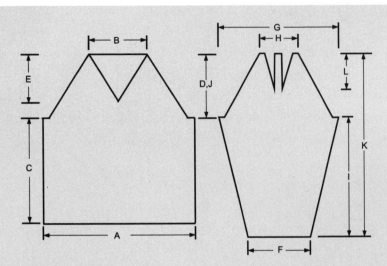

Finished Size: Garment measures 38 (42.5, 45.5, 50)" at chest and is 24.5 (25, 25.5, 26)" long.

Finished Measurements:

A. Back/front bottom width = 19 (21.25, 22.75, 25)"

B. Neck width = 7.75 (8.5, 9, 9.5)"

C. Body length = 15"

D. Armhole length = 8.5 (9, 9.5, 10)"

E. Front neck depth = 6 (6.75, 7, 7.75)"

F. Sleeve width at bottom = 8.5 (9, 9.5, 10)"

G. Sleeve width at upper arm = 15 (16.5, 17.5, 19)"

H. Sleeve width at top = 2"

I. Sleeve length to underarm = 17"

J. Sleeve "cap" = 8.5 (9, 9.5, 10)"

K. Total sleeve length = 25.5 (26, 26.5, 27)"

L. Sleeve dart depth = 4.5"

Materials:

- Patons "Classic Wool" (100% merino wool, 100g, appx 223yds/204m): 3 (3, 4, 4) skeins #212 Eggplant [color A], 3 (3, 3, 4) skeins #241 Hunter [color B], and 1 (2, 2, 2) skeins #239 Gold [color C].
- Size 5 knitting needles, or whatever size it takes to get the gauge.
- 16" circular knitting needles one size smaller than straight needles used.
- Stitch markers.

Gauge: 22 sts and 26 rows = 4" in Striped Rib pattern st after steam blocking.

Special Note: Slip-slip-knit = [slip next st as if to knit] twice, insert the left-hand needle from left to right through the fronts of these 2 sts, then knit the two together in this position [through their back loops].

Empire-Waisted, Sleeveless, A-Line, V-Neck Dress

(instructions p. 4)

Log Cabin Baby Blanket

(instructions p. 11)

Apron Front Halter Top

(instructions p. 16)

Ribbed Scarf, Hat, and Mittens

(instructions p. 23)

Easy, Reversible, Two-Toned Scarf (or Stole)

(instructions p. 31)

Lace Capelet

(instructions p. 36)

Cardi-Jacket

(instructions p. 44)

Lattice Pullover

(instructions p. 54)

Unisex Garter-Striped Diagonal Vest

(instructions p. 61)

Buttonless Evening Cardi-Jacket

(instructions p. 68)

A Trio of Pillows: Chenille Pillow, Slip-Stitch Pillow, and Aran Pillow

(instructions p. 75, 76, and 77)

Sleeveless Tank Top/Vest

(instructions p. 82)

Bulky, Boxy, Seamless Pullover

(instructions p. 88)

Man's Raglan-Sleeved Pullover Tunic

(instructions p. 94)

Convertible Handbag

(instructions p. 102)

Beaded Evening Clutch

(instructions p. 107)

Sport and Evening Bras

(instructions p. 112)

Short-Sleeved Crop Top with Patterned Center Panel

(instructions p. 120)

A Trio of Shoes: Ballet Slippers or Mary Janes, Striped Espadrille, and Ribbed Slide

(instructions p. 127, 131, and 135)

A Slew of Socks

(instructions p. 142)

Striped Rib Pattern

Pattern is a repeating multiple of 10 sts with 5 extra sts added at end and 14 rows.

Instead of cutting off each color and rejoining later, carry colors not in use loosely along side edges. Cast on designated number of sts with color A.

Rows 1, 3, and 5 [Right Side]—work initial sts as specified, ★p 5, k 1, p 1, k 1, p 1, k 1; repeat from ★ across ending with p 5, then work the last sts as specified.

Rows 2, 4, and 6 [Wrong Side]—work initial sts as specified, ★k 5, p 1, k 1, p 1, k 1, p 1; repeat from ★ across ending with k 5, then work the last sts as specified.

Rows 7 and 9 [Right Side]—change to B and work as for Row 1.

Row 8 [Wrong Side]—continue with B and work as for Row 2.

Row 10 [Wrong Side]—change to C and work initial sts as specified, p across, then work the last sts as specified.

Row 11 [Right Side]—continue with C and work as for Row 1.

Row 12 [Wrong Side]—change back to B and work initial sts as specified, p across, then work the last sts as specified—in essence, repeat Row 10.

Row 13 [Right Side]—continue with B and work as for Row 1.

Row 14 [Wrong Side]—continue with B and work as for Row 2.

Change to A and repeat Rows 1 through 14 for pattern.

In essence, k the k sts and p the p sts once pattern has been established except for Rows 9 and 11; just change colors in a sequence of ★6 rows A, 3 rows B, 2 rows C, then 3 rows B and repeat from ★.

Back

With color A, cast on 107 (119, 127, 139) sts. Begin with the Right Side row and k the first 2 sts as selvedges or end sts for a neater edge and for ease in seaming up later, [p 1, k 1] 2 (0, 2, 0) times, begin Striped Rib pattern over center 95 (115, 115, 135) sts, [k 1, p 1] 2 (0, 2, 0) times, end with k the last 2 sts again as selvedges. On the Wrong Side row, p the first 2 sts, [k 1, p 1] 2 (0, 2, 0) times, continue the Striped Rib pattern over the center 95 (115, 115, 135) sts, [p 1, k 1] 2 (0, 2, 0) times, and p the last 2 sts.

Work in this manner until piece measures 15" total, end ready to work a Right Side row or Row 1 of Striped Rib pattern. You will find it necessary to break off B and C at this point and rejoin as needed later.

Next row [Right Side]—with A, bind off 4 (6, 8, 10) sts, k next st, continue in established pattern to the end—there are 103 (113, 119, 129) sts.

Next row [Wrong Side]—bind off 4 (6, 8, 10) sts, p next st, continue in established pattern to within the last 2 sts, p the last 2 sts—there are 99 (107, 111, 119) sts.

Shape raglan armholes:

Next row or the Right Side—keep to Striped Rib pattern at all times and at the beginning of the row, k 1, slip-slip-knit the next 2 sts together to decrease, work in pattern to within the last 3 sts, k the next 2 sts together for another decrease, k the last st—there are 97 (105, 109, 117) sts.

Next row or the Wrong Side—p the first and last 2 sts and continue the Striped Rib pattern in between.

Repeat the last 2 rows (with 2 less sts for each set of the 2 rows) 26 (28, 29, 31) more times. Bind off the remaining 45 (49, 51, 55) sts, in pattern, ending off the remaining yarns.

Front

Work as for Back until there are 85 (93, 97, 105) sts on a Wrong Side row of armhole shaping. Mark center st.

Next row [Right Side]—continue in pattern with armhole decreases but after working first 41 (45, 47, 51) sts, bind off the next center st, then continue the row in pattern to the end—41 (45, 47, 51) sts remain at each shoulder.

Shape front V-neck:

Place the sts of right shoulder [the first set of 41 (45, 47, 51) sts with Wrong Side facing you] onto a st holder to be worked later. With Wrong Side facing you, join new balls of yarn as needed and work the Wrong Side row of left shoulder.

Next row, a Right Side row—continue the decreases at the beginning of the row for armhole shaping and work in pattern to within the last 3 sts at end of this shoulder, k the next 2 sts together for neck decrease, k the last st—39 (43, 45, 49) sts remain.

Next row or the Wrong Side—p the first and last 2 sts and continue the Striped Rib pattern in between.

Repeat the last 2 rows (with 2 less sts for each set of the 2 rows) 18 (20, 21, 23) more times. Bind off the remaining 3 sts, end off the remaining yarns.

Place the sts of right shoulder back onto the needles, ready to work a Wrong Side row. Join new balls of yarn as needed and work the Wrong Side row of right shoulder.

Repeat the 2 rows of the left shoulder in same manner, reversing the shaping, to complete this shoulder in identical fashion.

Sleeves

With color A, cast on 49 (51, 55, 57) sts.

Begin with the Right Side row and k the first 2

sts as selvedges, place a st marker on the needle and slip it as you work, begin with a partial pattern thus:

Size Small—k 1, [p 1, k 1] twice; size Medium—[p 1, k 1] 3 times; size Large—[p 1, k 1] 3 times; size Extra Large—p 3, [p 1, k 1] 3 times. Begin Striped Rib pattern over next center 35 sts, end with another partial pattern thus:

Size Small—[k 1, p 1] twice, k 1; size Medium—[k 1, p 1] 3 times; size Large—[k 1, p 1] 3 times, p 2; size Extra Large—[k 1, p 1] 3 times, p 3; place another st marker on the needle, then k the last 2 sts, again as selvedges.

On the Wrong Side row, p the first 2 and the last 2 sts and continue the Striped Rib pattern as established.

Continue in patterns as established and *at the same time,* increase 1 st at each end after the first marker and before the last marker on the Right Side rows on the 5th row, then on every 4th row 0 (10, 12, 21) more times, then on every 6th row 17 (10, 9, 3) more times, incorporating each increased st into the pattern and always maintaining the first and last 2 selvedge sts in Stockinette [k on Right Side rows, p on Wrong Side rows]. Each increase row will add 2 more sts to the total.

Work even in pattern on 85 (93, 99, 107) sts until sleeve measures 17" total, end ready to work a Right Side row or Row 1 of pattern and remove the prior st markers. You will find it necessary to break off B and C at this point and rejoin as needed later.

Next row [Right Side]—with A, bind off 4 (6, 8, 10) sts, k next st, continue in established pattern to the end—there are 81 (87, 91, 97) sts.

Next row [Wrong Side]—bind off 4 (6, 8, 10) sts, p next st, continue in established pattern to within the last 2 sts, p the last 2 sts—there are 77 (81, 83, 87) sts.

Shape raglan cap:

Next row or the Right Side—keep to Striped Rib pattern at all times and at the beginning of the row, k 1, slip-slip-knit the next 2 sts together to decrease, work in pattern to within the last 3 sts, k the next 2 sts together for another decrease, k the last st—there are 75 (79, 81, 85) sts.

Next row or the Wrong Side—p the first and last 2 sts and continue the Striped Rib pattern in between.

Repeat the last 2 rows (with 2 less sts for each set of the 2 rows) 11 (13, 14, 16) more times—there are 53 sts on a Wrong Side row. Mark the center 3 sts.

Shape shoulder dart:

★Next row [Right Side]—maintaining pattern, decrease for armhole, work to 2 sts before marked center 3 sts, k the next 2 sts together, [p 1, k 1, p 1] the next 3 sts to keep to pattern, slip-slip-knit the next 2 sts together, then continue the row in pattern to the end working armhole decrease—49 sts remain.

Next row or the Wrong Side—p the first 2 selvedge sts and continue the Striped Rib pattern up to within 1 st of marked center 3 sts, p 1, then k 1, p 1, k 1 the center 3 sts, p 1, continue the Striped Rib pattern to the last 2 sts and p the last 2 selvedge sts.

Next row or the Right Side—continue the decreases for raglan armholes and continue the Striped Rib pattern up to within 1 st of the first marker, k 1, slip marker, p 1, k 1, p 1, slip marker, k 1, continue the Striped Rib pattern to the last 3 sts and continue the decreases for raglan armholes—47 sts remain.

Repeat the last 2 rows, then repeat the Wrong Side row again.★

Repeat from ★ to ★ 4 more times.

Bind off the remaining 13 sts, in pattern, ending off the remaining yarns.

Finishing

Block pieces to measurements. Using mattress seaming [with Right Sides facing each other, insert sewing needle between the edge st and the next st in and pick up 2 bars, or "ladders," between the stitches alternately from each side], sew raglan shoulder seams and sew side and sleeve seams.

Neck trim:

With Right Side facing you, and using 16" circular knitting needles one size smaller than that used for sweater and color C, pick up and k 43 (47, 49, 53) sts from back neck (you've eliminated the end selvedge sts in mattress seaming), pick up the 11 sts of left sleeve, then pick up and k in each of the 40 (44, 46, 50) rows of left neck edge, skip center bound-off st, pick up and k in each of the 40 (44, 46, 50) rows of right neck edge, end with picking up the 11 sts of right sleeve—145 (157, 163, 175) sts. Place a st marker onto needle to mark beginning/end of row. With Right Side still facing you and working in rounds in a circle, p across all sts, decreasing at the center of V by purling together the 2 sts at bottom of each neck edge—144 (156, 162, 174) sts. With Right Side still facing you, bind off all sts around in knit.

:::: Convertible Handbag | Mirjana Kasap

CITY: Washington, DC

AGE: 25

Lily M. Chin

Mirjana lives in the nation's capital and loves the way that sounds—very important, as is everything else in Washington, D.C. She moved to the United States seven years ago from her native Croatia. She was raised in a beautiful coastal city, Split (no, it does not mean anything in her language).

She immigrated here because of the war in her country. When she first arrived, it was as an exchange student for her senior year of high school. She deemed it by far the worst year of her life. This was mostly because she did not get enough training on the issue of culture shock. Having been raised on the Adriatic in a city built in A.D. 303 (yes, that is 1,700 years ago), landing in a small town in Arizona near the Mexican border was more than she could handle.

When she graduated from high school she moved to Portland, Oregon, where she got a degree in international relations. After five years, though, she decided that she'd had enough of gray, rainy days. She moved to D.C. in 1998 just to see what life on the East Coast was like. So far she's loving it, since it reminds her of her life at home in Split, Croatia.

She is working as an international program manager for a cosmetic trade organization, but she is currently waiting to see if she got accepted into law school. She finds it a really annoying thing to do—wait, that is.

Unlike some of the other HYUKs, Mirjana (pronounced Meer-ee-AH-na) started knitting only about a year ago. She is hoping knitting is in her genes, however, since her eighty-two-year-old grandmother still knits and sends Mirjana intricate and complex socks and slippers so that her feet will not get cold. Mirjana says this practice is an old Eastern European tradition; there, they believe that if your feet are cold, you will get all kinds of ailments.

The person solely responsible for getting Mirjana knitting is her American "adoptive mom," Kathryn Gearheard. Kathryn is a whiz knitter and can make anything. When Kathryn heard about this project she thought it would be a great experience for Mirjana. Mirjana says, "As with most mothers, Kathryn was right."

Mirjana is six feet tall, which means that she frequently has to tell people she does not play basketball nor is she a model (though she *does* look like one).

Inspiration

Mirjana had her heart set on a designer-style bag à la Gucci, Chanel, or Ferragamo. She also wanted to use chunky yarn for this project for quick and easy knitting. She reminded me of her beginner/novice status.

A handbag should not stretch, so I chose a cotton and a cotton/viscose blend. They are both double-knitting weights. To "plump up" the yarn and get a heavier weight, I had Mirjana work with a strand of each yarn held together. Seed stitch is a good idea for someone just starting out in knitting. It is easy to work and to remember. It also imparts a wonderful texture that shows off the marled, two-tone effect of yarn mixes. Seed stitch has the added advantage of lying flat so there is no need for borders or trims. Gold is Mirjana's favorite color, and in these yarns, the sheen really comes out.

To stiffen the fabric and make the handbag hold up well, I had Mirjana work in a tighter tension than is normal. Mirjana had very specific ideas of what this handbag should look like and sent sketches with dimensions. The new, longer proportions are so modern. I loved her ideas for an interior pocket to hold a cell phone or car keys, and the detachable strap, not to mention tuckable handles to create a clutch. What a great way to use the gauge swatch too! The overall concept is so versatile.

She wrote: "I want to make a bag that is going to have a dual purpose. I want it to be a day bag for a businesswoman who needs a nice accessory with her briefcase, and I want it to be an easy-to-carry evening bag that will be the perfect accessory with that little black dress we all have. I envision using handles for daytime (necessitating small handles) with a detachable strap that attaches with two buttons on the side. In the evening, the handles can just sort of slide in and be invisible. Remove the strap and the bag becomes a clutch. Every fashionable bag should have a cell phone holder. I do not want it to be visible, though, so I would like to place the cell phone pocket on the inside, hidden away. Also, should we consider lining this bag?"

A lining definitely helps. The easy way is to use iron-on, nonwoven fusible interfacing. A more elegant way is to use a stiff silk and sew it in. Or do what Ingrid (see page 107) did with her bag and use both. I leave these as options. For such slippery yarns, try Aurora's line of bamboo Drops needles. The great handles are a specialty of Judi & Co. (they also do a line of their own handbags).

⚡ **Instructions** | Convertible Handbag

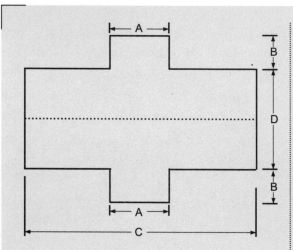
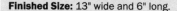

Finished Size: 13" wide and 6" long.

Finished Measurements:

- **A.** Handle wrap width = 3"
- **B.** Handle wrap depth = 2"
- **C.** Bag body width = 13"
- **D.** Full bag body length = 12"

Materials:

- Aurora/Garnstudio "Cotton Viscose" (54% cotton, 46% viscose, 50g, appx 109yds): 2 skeins #004 Gold.
- Aurora/Garnstudio "Muskat" (100% Egyptian cotton, 50g, appx 109yds): 2 skeins #30 Yellow.
- Size 6 knitting needles, or whatever size it takes to get the gauge.
- Judi & Co.'s D-shaped bag handles, 4" without holes in Buttercrunch, 4" wide and about 3" high.
- Three 7/8" buttons.
- Optional: iron-on, nonwoven fusible interfacing and/or stiff silk for lining.

Gauge: 20 sts and 32 rows = 4" in Seed st. (If you make your swatch about 5" × 3" it will also double as interior pocket for cell phone. Cast on 25 sts and work for 3", check gauge, bind off, leaving 20" tail for sewing.)

Special Notes: Work with a strand of A and a strand of B held together throughout. Bag is worked all in one piece from top to bottom. Firmer than usual tension is used for sturdiness.

First handle wrap:

With a strand of A and B held together, cast on 15 sts, leaving a 16" tail at the beginning for sewing later. Work Seed st (★k 1, p 1; repeat from ★ across, end k 1 every row—basically, k the p sts and p the k sts as they present themselves) for 2".

Body:

Cast on 25 sts at the beginning of the next 2 rows, keeping new sts in Seed st pattern by beginning with p 1. Work on 65 sts until body portion measures 11.5".

Next row, buttonhole row—work Seed st

over next 31 sts, bind off next center 3 sts for buttonhole, work Seed st over remainder of sts.

Next row—work to bound-off sts, cast on 3 sts, work remainder of row. Continue in pattern until body portion measures 12" total.

Second handle wrap:

Bind off 25 sts at the beginning of the next 2 rows. Work on 15 sts until handle wrap measures 2", then bind off, leaving an 8" tail for sewing.

Finishing

If more body or stiffness is desired, cut a piece of nonwoven, fusible interfacing to fit over piece, leaving ¼" from edges for seaming. Iron onto one side and designate this as inside or Wrong Side of piece. Fold body in half lengthwise with Right Sides facing each other and sew side seams. Turn piece inside out. Slide handle wrap through opening of each purchased Handle from outside to inside. Fold over and sew across insides or Wrong Sides of bag, on level of where body begins/ends. Sew 1 button to inside of bag opposite buttonhole.

Strap:

Make twisted cord by cutting 4 strands each of A and B, each 3 yards long. Knot these together 1" from each end. If you have someone to help you, insert a pencil or knitting needle through each end of the strands. If not, place one end over a doorknob or drawer handle and put a pencil through the other end. Holding the yarn tightly, turn the strands clockwise until they are tightly twisted. They should begin to kink slightly. Then, keeping the strands taut, fold the piece in half. You may find a heavy, dangling clip-on item that's easily removable (such as a set of keys) helpful by placing it in the center to weigh the middle down before drawing the ends together. Remove the pencils and allow the cord to twist onto itself. Adjust end knots as desired. Form loops big enough for buttons at either end and tack down. Sew buttons to either end of opening at top edge of bag, for attaching strap.

Interior Pocket for Cell Phone:

Take swatch and position it against an interior side of bag at any place desired. Use tail end to invisibly sew down (so that it's not seen on outside) 3 edges, keeping top edge open.

⇒ **Beaded Evening Clutch** | Ingrid M. Case

Lily M. Chin

CITY: Minneapolis, MN
AGE: 32

Ingrid lives in Minneapolis with her husband and two cats. During most of the day she's a financial and business writer and editor.

Ingrid learned embroidery, crochet, and needlepoint as a child from her mother and grandmother, but didn't take up knitting until about four years ago, when a Czech friend taught her how. Ingrid rapidly became addicted and started reading books on knitting. Even though Zuzana is back in Prague, the nasty little habit she taught Ingrid lives on. Ingrid mostly knits sweaters, some of her own design and some from commercial patterns.

Inspiration

Ingrid thought of beaded bags and accessories and said, "They're easy and fun and not the least bit grandmothery. I know the yarn is fine-gauge, but these are such small projects that the time required to make one is not huge. They're not prohibitively expensive, either. Beading looks fancy but is dead easy once you've tried it for a bead or two."

She is so right. They're hot, versatile, doable and addictive. I know. I've gone to town with beaded knitting myself. Traditionally worked in silk or cotton thread with small needles, beaded knitting is just like any other knitting but smaller, with extra stuff hanging off the yarn! If you can knit and purl, you can knit with beads.

There are magnifying tools that hang from the neck to aid the eyesight if need be. They are found at shops that specialize in needlepoint or embroidery, or even at some yarn stores and art and craft suppliers. Good lighting is a must. The size of the needles may take a little getting used to, but they're still the same pointy sticks we're all familiar with.

Sturdy cotton is necessary because the beads are strung onto the yarn. As you knit, you must continually shove the beads farther down along the yarn. This is why Ingrid suggests not placing too many beads on all at once. Cut the yarn and restring often instead.

This method of applying beads is one of the simplest. The beads just lie on the strand of yarn *between* the stitches. When you want to place a bead, just bring it up on the yarn and snuggle it close to the needle before working the next stitch. The beads show best on Reverse Stockinette stitch, which is precisely what Ingrid used.

I loved the composition Ingrid came up with. Geometrics hold such universal appeal. More importantly, they are easier to work than more irregular shapes. Ingrid writes, "The chart may look intimidating. Just remember that each square is as many beads high as it is wide and you'll find it easy to alter the pattern, either to fix a mistake or because you found a better way to do it!" It's also important to remember that the beads are only put into place every *other* row or every knit row. The chart only represents the knit rows—purl rows are not shown.

Ingrid's ideas for other beaded projects include a drawstring bag, beaded gloves, a beaded choker or ankle bracelet that ties in the back, a bookmark, or even the trim on a sweater. This cotton comes in plenty of colors to choose from. Our bag would be a great bridal accessory done in white with gold or pearl beads.

Chart your ideas on graph paper to plan bead placement. I find it helps to draw through the chart with a highlighter marker after working that row. This keeps your place and it underlines the next row to be worked. Stick to one bead color first, as color patterns must be strung on in exact reverse order of appearance (i.e., the last bead on is the first one knit).

Ingrid says, "This bag was a fun challenge, and not something I would have attempted without this book as a rationale."

Instructions | Beaded Evening Clutch

Finished Size: The entire bag, spread flat, is 14" long. The body of the bag is 10.5" wide and 9.5" long. The top flap is 9" wide and 3.5" long.

Materials:

- Caron "Grandma's Best" (100% mercerized cotton crochet thread, style 276A, size 10, 350 yds): 1 skein #63 Burgundy.
- 7000 or 7 oz size six gold glass beads.
- Size 000 knitting needles.
- One transparent plastic snap.
- Optional: 3/8 yard lining fabric (here, marigold-colored raw silk dupioni).
- Optional: 3/8 yard interfacing (here, heavyweight, nonfusable interfacing in white).
- Optional: Thread for sewing lining (here, YLI silk thread in #30).

Gauge: 38 sts and 64 rows = 4" over the beaded chart pattern. Note, however, that gauge isn't crucial on this project. If you want a smaller or larger bag, that's up to you.

Special Notes: To put beads on yarn: Use a small, blunt-point tapestry needle. Thread the needle and slide the beads down and onto the yarn. It's easiest if you "load" only about 100 to 200 beads at a time. When you run out of beads, break yarn at the end of a row, rethread beads, and continue on.

Bead placement method: Beads are placed on the running threads between stitches. To place a bead, bring it to the working end of your yarn, against the fabric. Knit the next stitch. Repeat. Beads show best on the Reverse Stockinette side of the fabric, so this bag presents the purl side as the public side. You could achieve a much more subtle effect by making the Stockinette side the public side.

Bag

Cast on 99 sts and work 8 rows in Garter stitch [knit all rows]. Switch to Reverse Stockinette stitch [p Right Side rows, k Wrong Side rows] and follow the chart for bead placement. *Note that the chart shows only knit rows and the bead is placed before knitting the marked boxes.* Place beads on every knit row; purl back on every purl row.

When you reach the appropriate place on the chart, bind off 7 stitches at the beginning of the next 2 rows to begin creating the bag's flap closure. Continue with the chart, keeping the first and last five stitches of each row in Garter stitch so the edges of the flap lie flat. When you reach the end of the beading chart, work 8 rows in Garter stitch. Bind off in Garter stitch.

Finishing

Block the bag. If you wish to line it, do so before sewing it together. Ingrid put the bag together as follows: Cut a piece of interfacing to the same size as the bag and cut a piece of silk that is one inch larger than the bag on each side. Fold the extra silk to the back of the interfacing and stitch the interfacing to the silk using a hand backstitch. Attach the two sides of the bag's body lining using that same stitch, and then sew the lining to the bag using a hand hemstitch.

At this point, or if you've decided not to line your handbag, fold the bag so that the Right Sides of the body are facing each other and the flap is hanging out at the top by itself. Pin the sides in place. Backstitch the side seams of the body together. Turn the bag Right Side out and sew a snap to the top and center of the bag.

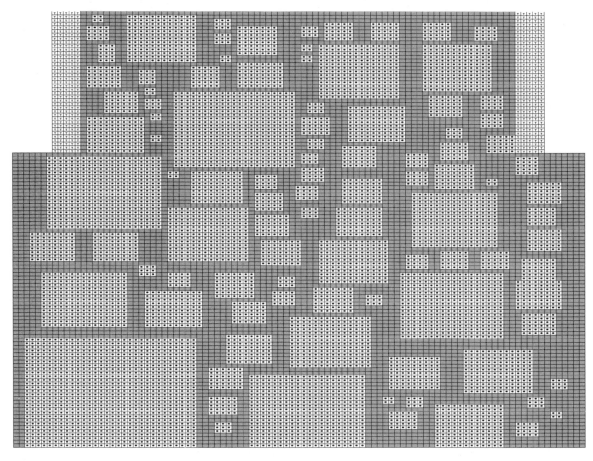

The Urban Knitter

Raphael Baruch

✿ **Sport and Evening Bras** | Lori Monaco

CITY: Miami, FL
AGE: 38

Lori's grandmother always knitted when she was a girl, but she taught Lori to crochet because she was afraid Lori would poke her eyes out with the knitting needles! Lori's friend Chantal taught her to knit when they were both pregnant with their first children—yes, pregnant women knitting booties, they're sorry to say!

Luckily, Chantal is of German origin so Lori learned to knit continental right from the start. As soon as she got the basics down, she proceeded to knit her way through many nights in front of the "tube" but now most of her knitting is done in airports and on planes.

Lori is a chartered financial analyst by profession and heads up the research department for a Miami-based investment bank. She travels to Latin America to visit with media and telecom companies to determine appropriate investments for the bank's clients.

Knitting in public (or kipping, as knitters on the Internet call it) has its moments—mostly pleasant ones as the work acts as a bridge between cultures and overcomes language barriers.

"Knitting keeps me sane—with the possible exception of ripping mohair lace patterns," Lori says. "I have to admit that I am a selfish knitter. I knit primarily for myself and my two sons, Julien and Stephane. I just can't bear to part with my work—so much of my thoughts, experiences, and emotions gets tangled up in the stitches. Knitting is now a part of me and an infinite number of projects live and grow in my head, cued up waiting for my fingers to set them free."

Inspiration

Lori originally thought it would be interesting to do two tops—one very sporty for "watersports" activities, and the other for evening wear with beads.

Her list of essential design elements included: close-fitting top, ability to wear a regular bra underneath, shaping via darts, elastic band for snug closure, firm closure included in design so it does not have to be sewn in, and knit in one piece if possible. She also thought it would be a nice idea to include a formula for sizing a fitted top and to include possible modifications to the design.

While working out the directions for Lori's bra, I realized I'd just about stumbled onto the equivalent of the cure for the common cold! Well, not quite. For women, one of those impossible-dream quests has always been to find that Perfect-Fitting Bra. If I'm not mistaken, the following instructions may very well get you there! The cups take maybe an evening and the piece is small so it goes pretty quickly.

In essence, this is a real, true bra. Some influence came from crocheted bikinis, of which I've made many commercially. This kind of construction has been used in crochet for years, so why not translate it into knit?

I made a few slight deviations from Lori's stipulations. For one thing, this *is* the bra you can wear underneath things! Also, I found that sewn closures give the most flexibility. However, while there are pieces worked separately, sewing is still minimal.

In addition, the fronts have extended tabs that overlap like a mini surplice. This acts to "lift and separate," as they say. Many opportunities for size adjustments are inherent (i.e., to let the breasts be further apart or closer together). Also, since you can wear this innerwear as outerwear there's a little less cleavage this way. Inspiration came from my own front-closure, wrap-around bra.

Finally, stitch and direction of knitting allows for four-way stretch and will mold and conform easily to any bosom type. It also creates great-looking, dynamic lines.

Lori also wrote a list of potential modifications of the original design:

- Some type of scallop stitch on top of bra cup like a picot edge
- I-cord trim
- Knit some beads directly into the garment
- Have bottom beads be detachable for ease of laundering and have them set on an elasti-

cized band as well. Another possible way to attach could be via snaps or hooks and eyes on the inside bottom edge.

- Instead of k 2, p 2 Ribbing, the body of the fabric can be a simple lace eyelet, or any number of designs—just as long as it has some body to it.

While I've not included these in the directions, certainly any knitter with some experience can add and alter to suit her taste. Come to think of it, I have a friend who is a Middle Eastern dancer who would love the metallic version as part of her costume. I can spangle it and apply all kinds of froufrou. . . .

The yarns are perfect as this cotton/acrylic blend stretches and bounces and molds to curves well. The metallic is silky and not itchy. It is slippery, though. For this reason, I highly recommend the Addi Natura® needles from Skacel. They are made of bamboo, which prevents too much sliding around.

Instructions | Sport and Evening Bras

Cross-front with back-closure

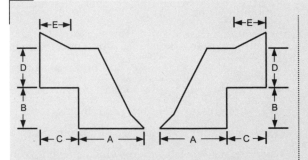

Finished Size: Garment is intended for 30–32 (34–36, 38–40)" bust measurement with B to C cup size. If you are an A cup, you can consider making one size smaller and steam block the dickens out of it. If you are larger than a C cup, make the next largest size or use a needle size larger or increase as per notes.

Finished Measurements:

A. Bottom of beginning cup portion = 4 (5, 6)"
B. Height of beginning cup portion = 2.5 (3, 3.5)"
C. Picked-up sts = same as height of beginning cup portion = 2.5 (3, 3.5)"
D. Height of side cup portion = 2.5 (3, 3.5)"
E. Side tab extension = 0.75 (2, 2.5)"

Materials:

- Skacel "Polo" (60% cotton, 40% acrylic, 50g, appx 153yds): 2 skeins #55 French Vanilla or Skacel "Karat" (90% rayon, 10% polyester metallic, 50g, appx 143 yds): 2 skeins.
- Knitting needles in sizes 2 and 4 or whatever sizes it takes to get the gauges. We recommend the Addi Natura® bamboo needles also from Skacel.
- Knitting needles one size smaller than the largest of the two selected above.
- ³⁄₄" nonroll elastic, long enough to go around rib cage and then some.
- Matching thread and sewing needle, safety pins, straight pins.
- Hook closure (we used skirt hooks and eyes from Prym, article #26802).

Gauge: 24 sts and 48 rows = 4" in Giant Garter pattern on smallest needles. 20 sts = 4" in Stockinette st on largest needles. In essence, these are double-knitting-weight yarns worked on a slightly tightened tension, then on a slightly loosened tension.

Giant Garter Pattern

Pattern is a 6-row repeat worked over any number of sts.

Row 1, a Wrong Side row—slip first st with yarn in front, bring yarn to the back in order to k, k across.

Row 2, a Right Side row—slip first st with yarn in front, p across.

Row 3—slip first st with yarn in back as if to k, k across.

Rows 4 through 6—repeat Rows 1 through 3.

Repeat Rows 1 through 6 for pattern.

Notice how the slipping at beginning of rows forms a nice and tidy side-chain.

Right Cup

With smallest needles, cast on 26 (32, 38) sts.

Begin Giant Garter pattern *but*:

On Row 2, a Right Side row, mark beginning as center edge and decrease after slipping first st—25 (31, 37) sts. Continue in pattern and decrease at this center edge in same manner every other row 2 (5, 8) more times, then every 4th row 6 times.

For D cups and larger: *At same time*, increase 1 st in 2nd-to-last st at left-hand edge when Right Side is facing you, every 6th row 4 (5, 6) times.

For all sizes: End with row 30 (36, 42) and 17 (20, 23) sts or 21 (25, 29) sts for D cups and larger.

Do *not* turn row, Right Side is still facing you. Instead, bring yarn over the needle in a knitwise fashion to create an extra st at the corner, then along side edge, pick up and k 1 st for each of the 15 (18, 21) chains. It will be slightly tight, I know, but it will pass quickly as you gain more rows—33 (39, 45) sts or 37 (44, 51) sts for D cups and larger.

Continue in pattern and continue to decrease at center edge every 4th row as before until another 31 (37, 43) rows have been completed for a total of 61 (73, 85) rows—25 (30, 34) sts or 29 (35, 40) sts for D cups and larger.

Side extensions:

Next row [Right Side]—continue in pattern and bind off first 13 (15, 17) sts or 17 (20, 23) sts for D cups and larger, complete row—12 (15, 17) sts remain for all cup sizes.

Work a Wrong Side row.

Next row [Right Side]—decrease after slipping first st—11 (14, 16) sts.

Continue in pattern and repeat last 2 rows until 3 sts remain.

Next row—k 3 sts together, end off.

Left Cup

With smaller needles, cast on 26 (32, 38) sts.

Begin Giant Garter pattern *but*:

On Row 2, a Right Side row, work to 3 sts of end, decrease, then work last st—25 (31, 37) sts. Mark this decreased edge as center edge. Continue in pattern and decrease at this center edge in same manner every other row 2 (5, 8) more times, then every 4th row 6 times.

For D cups and larger: *At same time*, increase 1 st in 2nd st from right-hand edge when Right Side is facing you, every 6th row 4 (5, 6) times.

For all sizes: End with row 29 (35, 41) and 17 (20, 23) sts or 21 (25, 29) sts for D cups and larger. End off yarn!

With Right Side facing you, rejoin yarn to bottom of right side edge [the straight edge]. Pick up and k 1 st for each of the 15 (18, 21) chains, bring yarn over the needle in a knitwise fashion to create an extra st at the corner, then finish off row 30 (36, 42)—33 (39, 45) sts or 37 (44, 51) sts for D cups and larger.

Continue in pattern and continue to decrease at center edge every 4th row as before until another 32 (38, 44) rows have been completed for a total of 62 (74, 86) rows—25 (30, 34) sts or 29 (35, 40) sts for D cups and larger.

Side extensions:

Next row [Wrong Side]—continue in pattern and bind off first 13 (15, 17) sts or 17 (20, 23) sts for D cups and larger, complete row—12 (15, 17) sts remain for all cup sizes.

Next row [Right Side]—work to within 3 sts of end, decrease, then work last st—11 (14, 16) sts.

Work a Wrong Side row.

Continue in pattern and repeat last 2 rows until 3 sts remain.

Next row—k 3 sts together, end off.

Straps

With smaller needles and Right Side facing you, pick up and k 5 (5, 7) sts at top of each cup along last decrease rows of center edge.

Row 1 [Wrong Side]—slip first st as if to purl with yarn in front, ★k 1, p 1; repeat from ★.

Row 2 [Right Side]—slip first st as if to knit with yarn in back, ★p 1, k 1; repeat from ★.

Repeat Rows 1 and 2 until straps are way longer than you think is necessary [fitting over the shoulder to midback] and you're sick of them, bind off.

Fitting

Here comes the exciting part. Enlist the aid of a really good friend or competent loved one. Begin by wrapping elastic below bust and pin closed, making sure it's neither too loose nor too tight. Remember, this will help support you as well.

Now grab each respective cup and begin to pin to elastic. You will have to adjust fit according to your needs and may have to try several times for just the right fit. Overlap the center as much or as little as you need/want. For larger cup sizes, try shirring the bottoms of the cups for more fullness using needle and thread. Don't forget to lengthen or shorten straps and tack them down to back of elastic.

When all is done, *very carefully* mark off onto elastic the point where straps should be in back, the point where each side of cups begins, and the point where cup fronts overlap. Now before you take this off, measure the elastic around. This should be the same measurement as your rib cage.

Measure how far it is to each of the marked-off points [e.g., 6" from center-back to strap, another 5" from strap to beginning of cup, cups span center front 16" total with 3" overlap in middle, etc.] and write these down. Now you can disassemble. If you've gathered or shirred the cups any, don't take out the gathers or shirring. Try and keep the cups together with the overlap intact.

Bottom band:

OK, now we have to do our own individual math for a moment, but don't panic. This should not be difficult and it's short. First, we will use our Stockinette gauge on larger needles of 5 sts per inch. That's a nice, easy, round number.

A. Multiply the rib cage measurement just below bust by 5. What is this? _____ This will be the total number of sts for your bottom band. For example, 30" × 5 sts = 150 sts. See? That wasn't so bad, right?

B. Now, how many inches from center-back to beginning of cups? Multiply this by 5. What is this? _____ This will be the number of sts you cast on before picking up sts from bottom of cups.

C. How many inches is the full span of the cups? Multiply this by 5. What is this? _____

This will be the number of sts you have to pick up along the bottom of cups.

D. You'll have to cast on the same number as B for sts to cast on after cups.

   B + C + D = A, right? Do you get something close to A? Good.

Soooo, with Right Side facing you and using larger needles, cast on number of B sts, pick up and knit number of C sts along bottom edge of cups, evenly spaced, going through both thicknesses of fabric at front overlap, cast on number of D sts for a total of number of A sts.

Work in Stockinette for 1". *Change to one needle size smaller*, work a knit on Wrong Side or a purl on Right Side for turning ridge, then continue in Stockinette for another 1" or just a row short of 1". Fold band and sew open sts closed to Wrong Side. Insert elastic into tubing formed by fold. Tack ends in place to prevent sliding. Seam sides closed *or* fold back one side of elastic to form loop, sew ring fastener to other side of elastic . . . this will depend on what kind of closure you decide on. In a pinch, there are skirt hook and eyes that are flat metal.

Sew straps to back of band.

Variations: Continue a few more rows toward end of cups if you want more filled-in sides. This will move straps over a little toward outer shoulder, but you can then also have wider straps. For wider straps—just pick up more sts, making sure it's an *odd* number. I find picking up 2 sts per chain (or 1 per row, since each chain represents 2 rows) reduces stretching or puckering.

Short-Sleeved Crop Top with Patterned Center Panel

| Janica York

CITY: Birmingham, AL

AGE: 30

Janica was born in Huntsville, Alabama, home of Marshall Space Flight Center and NASA. Huntsville, although not the largest city in the state, is definitely one of the most cosmopolitan. The space program attracts highly educated people from around the world. She now lives in Birmingham, which is the largest city in the state and cosmopolitan in its own right.

Janica first learned to knit from her mother when she was five. When her mother, who's British, lived in the U.K. (she moved from Birmingham, England) every child was taught to knit in school. Janica remembers large wooden needles and a ball of hideous dark brown yarn. She didn't understand casting on, but could knit and purl for rows and rows once her mother got her started. Janica didn't keep up with it, however, and didn't knit again until it became an occupational necessity.

She received a degree with honors in English, with minors in art and business, from Birmingham-Southern College, a small liberal arts school with a reputation for strong academics. Janica spent six years in the publishing business editing craft books for Oxmoor House, primarily in crochet. In fact, she was the editor for my first book, a crochet book at that, *Mosaic Magic: Afghans Made Easy.*

Janica picked up yarn, hooks, and needles as if

she'd never stopped. She has edited books on quilting, though she's a self-proclaimed disaster with needles that have eyes in them. She's a certified crochet instructor with the Craft Yarn Council of America as well as a knitter.

She now works on publications in University Relations at Samford University, a private Christian school, also with a strong academic reputation. With nine schools comprising the university, the publications are numerous and varied, which keeps work challenging and interesting for her. She loves the communal feel of the college atmosphere. They have one of the prettiest campuses in the nation, and Janica says the people are amazing, both students and staff.

Inspiration

Living in the extremely hot and humid South, Janica likes knitting items that don't leave her sweating. Her two failings as a Southerner (which she is quite proud to be) are that she dislikes both the climate and iced tea.

She loves thick wool sweaters, but they just aren't practical there. So she was thrilled with the chance to design a lightweight top with a flattering shape for year-round wear.

One of Janica's favorite sweaters is a cropped little yellow sweater. It's lightweight, short-sleeved, and short, with a nice neckline. There is an overall horizontal pattern purled in. It's loose around the waist, which makes it great for wearing with jeans or khakis. "Cropped seems to work for some of us shorter folks," she proclaims.

She sent me the sweater and I took its vital statistics (i.e., all the dimensions). I wanted to recreate the overall shape and fit, but change some of the details.

Here were Janica's thoughts: a short-sleeved, cropped top with a fabulous neckline, in a lightweight fiber with a somewhat lacy pattern. (Not so lacy that you'd have to wear something under it for decency—layering certainly defeats the purpose of being cool enough for the South!). Many of the cottons available to her had been really stretchy, and this sweater needs to retain its shape. She trusted me implicitly on yarn choices for this.

She drew some preliminary pictures. I really liked the idea of a center panel, to appear slimming. Furthermore, stitch-interest would be focused on this center panel and the sides would remain plain for ease in knitting. The particular stitch-interest in this case happens to be lace, and keeping it in the front and center meant avoiding indiscreet placement at the full point of the bust.

Janica instantly fell in love with her yarn, including the name. She said, "How can you resist a yarn named 'Slinky'?" Indeed, it has both sheen and texture. This proved a little problematic as Janica swatched and swatched many lace patterns. Most did not show up well and fought with the slight nubbiness of the yarn. She loved the drape and feel of "Slinky" too much to give up, though, and it is lightweight and ideal for her climate. She chose a great copper color that goes beautifully with her carrot-top colorations.

Simplest turned out to be most effective, as is often the case. I suggested an easy yarn-over, knit-2-together eyelet across a row, separated by Garter ridges in rows in-between: violá. Not only is it pretty, it functions well. Since plain knitting is placed side by side with a stitch pattern, the row gauges must match lest a portion of the sweater become longer than the rest. Lace usually enlarges a row gauge, but the Garter ridges hike it back up. This resulted in a perfect match to the Stockinette sides.

I opted to keep "stitch integrity." This means no "fiddling" with the center panel pattern other than increasing the number of stitches. The decreases and general shaping all occur in the side sections of Stockinette and the center is left alone.

Do be careful when increasing the center panel, though. Make sure that every yarn-over is followed by a knit-2-together decrease. Where there is not enough stitches, omit the yarn-over altogether (unless you *want* to increase, in which case the yarn-over acts as an increased extra stitch). Again, match each yo with k2tog and you'll maintain proper stitch-count.

In all honesty, it's not the easiest pattern in this book, because several things are going on at the same time: side shaping, center shaping, then armhole shaping. For this reason, it's not a bad idea to draw out full stitch charts for your size. To do this, work with knitter's proportioned graph paper. Every box represents a stitch of the garment to be worked across and every row on the paper represents a row of knitting, to be worked from the bottom up. Thus, you will need sheets of graph paper with at least as many boxes as there are stitches and rows.

After laying down all the stitches and charting out both shapings and stitch patterns within these boxes, draw through the row just completed with a highlighter marker to help keep your place and to "underline" the next row you're working on.

Janica says one of the most frustrating things for HYUKs is that there is a plethora of simple patterns that don't really fit well, or well-fitting patterns so complicated that they become daunting. I hope this sweater fills the gap between.

Janica is practical at heart. Having worked in the crafts industry, she understood that some of the projects needed to be very accessible to the average knitter. Many HYUKs just want to get started on basic projects that have more flair than what you normally find. Funky colors and cool patterns could be just the thing. Yet the shape could be classic. She also promised me that Southern knitters will be thrilled!

Shaped and body-skimming

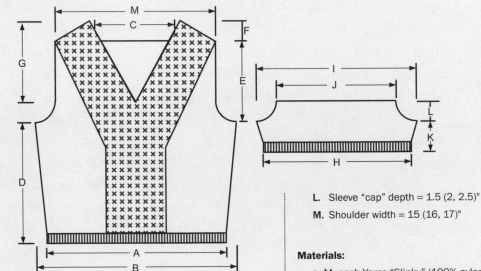

Finished Size: Garment measures 36 (40, 44)" at chest and is 19.5 (20, 20.5)" long.

Finished Measurements:

A. Back/front bottom waist = 15.5 (17.75, 19.5)"
B. Back/front bust = 18 (20, 22)"
C. Neck width = 5.75 (6, 6.5)"
D. Body length = 12"
E. Armhole length = 7.5 (8, 8.5)"
F. Front shoulder slope = 2"
G. Front neck depth = 6.75 (7, 7.5)"
H. Sleeve width bottom = 14 (15, 16)"
I. Sleeve width upper arm = 15 (16, 17)"
J. Sleeve width top = 12"
K. Sleeve depth to underarm = 3"

L. Sleeve "cap" depth = 1.5 (2, 2.5)"
M. Shoulder width = 15 (16, 17)"

Materials:

- Muench Yarns "Slinky" (100% nylon, 50g, appx 216yds): 5 (6, 6) skeins #20 Copper.
- Size 5 knitting needles, or whatever size it takes to get the gauge.
- Stitch markers.
- Stitch holder.

Gauge: 28 sts and 36 rows = 4" in Stockinette and in Staggered Eyelet pattern (a lacy pattern).

Special Notes: St markers help distinguish center panel of Staggered Eyelet pattern from Stockinette sides of knitting. Slip st markers as you work.

Slip-slip-knit = [slip next st as if to knit] twice, insert the left-hand needle from left to right through the fronts of these 2 sts, then knit the two together in this position [through their back loops].

Staggered Eyelet Pattern:

Pattern is worked over a multiple of 4 plus 3 sts.

Row 1 [a Right Side row]—k 3, ★yarn-over (or wrap yarn around the needle as if to knit), k 2 together, k 2; repeat from ★ across.

Rows 2, 4, 6 [Wrong Side rows]—p across.

Row 3 [a Right Side row]—p across.

Row 5 [a Right Side row]—k 1, ★yarn-over, k 2 together; k 2; repeat from ★ across, end with yarn-over, k 2 together.

Row 7 [a Right Side row]—p across.

Row 8 [Wrong Side row]—p across.

Repeat Rows 1 through 8 for Staggered Eyelet pattern.

Back

Cast on 111 (125, 139) sts.

Row 1, a Right Side row—k 1, ★p 1, k 1; repeat from ★ for Ribbing.

Row 2, a Wrong Side row—p 1, ★k 1, p 1; repeat from ★ for Ribbing.

Repeat last 2 rows until there are a total of 9 rows, end by finishing a Right Side row.

Begin side and center panels and patterns:

Next row [a Wrong Side row]—p 36 (41, 46), place stitch marker onto needle, p 39 (43, 47), place a second st marker, p 36 (41, 46).

Next row [a Right Side row]—k across.

Next row—p across.

Next row—continue to work Stockinette on both sides [k on Right Side, p on Wrong Side] and begin Staggered Eyelet pattern over center 39 (43, 47) sts.

Continue to work in patterns as established.

At the same time, shape for bust:

Next row or the Right Side—k 2, increase, work to within 2 sts from end, increase, k last 2 sts—113 (127, 141) sts.

Continue to increase in this manner every 10th row 7 more times—127 (141, 155) sts.

At the same time, shape center panel:

When piece measures 9.5" total from beginning, end ready to work a Right Side row.

Next row or the Right Side—k to within 3 sts of first marker, k 2 together, k 1, slip marker, maintaining pattern, increase, work center panel across and increase before next marker, slip marker, k 1, slip-slip-knit decrease, k to end—41 (45, 49) sts of Staggered Eyelet pattern and 1 less st on each side panel.

[Repeat this row every 4th row, then every 2nd row alternately] 14 (15, 16) times, then repeat this row every 4th row 1 (0, 0) more time. Incorporate increased-sts into maintaining Staggered Eyelet pattern. There are a total of 30 (31, 33) increased rows—99 (105, 113) sts of Staggered Eyelet pattern total.

At the same time, shape for armholes:

When work measures 12" total from beginning, end ready to work a Right Side row. There are still 127 (141, 155) sts.

Keeping to patterns, bind off 4 (6, 7) sts at the beginning of the next 2 rows—119 (129, 141) sts.

Next row [a Decrease row], worked on Right Side—k 2, k 2 together, work to within last 4 sts, slip-slip-knit decrease, k last 2 sts—117 (127, 139) sts.

Repeat last Decrease row on next 5 (7, 9) Right Side rows—107 (113, 121) sts.

Work even in established patterns until armholes measure 7.5 (8, 8.5)" total from the beginning of armhole shaping, end with a Wrong Side row. Bind off.

Front

Work same as for back until piece measures same as back to armholes.

Shape for armholes:

For size Small: Shape as for back armhole. When piece measures 1.75" from beginning of armhole shaping or 13.75" total, end ready to work a Right Side row.

Keeping to patterns, bind off dead-center st to divide for neck—106 sts or 53 sts on either side of dead center.

★   ★   ★

For sizes Medium and Large: Keeping to patterns, bind off (6, 7) sts at the beginning of the next 2 rows—(129, 141) sts.

Next row [a Decrease row], worked on Right Side—k 2, k 2 together, work to within last 4 sts, slip-slip-knit decrease, k last 2 sts— (127, 139) sts.

Repeat Decrease row on next 6 Right Side rows—(115, 127) sts.

Repeat Decrease row on next Right Side row but bind off dead-center st as well to divide for neck—(112, 124) sts or (56, 62) sts on either side of dead center.

For size Large only: Work Decrease rows at armhole edges on each of the next 2 Right Side rows *as you continue to shape for V-neck.*

Shape for V-neck (for all sizes):

Work a Wrong Side row over first 53 (56, 62) sts and place these sts of right shoulder onto a st holder to be worked later. Join another ball of yarn to left shoulder and work a Wrong Side row over these 53 (56, 62) sts.

Next row or the Right Side [a Decrease row]—k to within 3 sts of first marker, k 2 together, k 1, work center panel—32 (34, 36) sts of Staggered Eyelet pattern and 20 (21, 24) sts of side panel in Stockinette for 52 (55, 60) sts total.

Note: This Decrease row continues outward movement of center panel pattern.

All Wrong Side rows—p across.

Repeat Decrease row—51 (54, 58) sts total, 32 (34, 36) of Staggered Eyelet pattern and 19 (20, 22) sts of side panel in Stockinette.

Note: Decreases for armholes are now complete for size Large.

[Repeat Decrease row every 4th row, then every 2nd row alternately] 7 (8, 9) more times, then repeat Decrease row on next Right Side row 1 (0,0) more time. There are 36 (38, 40) sts at last Decrease row or 32 (34, 36) sts of Staggered Eyelet pattern and 4 sts of side panel in Stockinette.

Work even in patterns until armhole edge measures 7.5 (8, 8.5)" total from the beginning of armhole shaping, end with a Wrong Side row. Bind off.

Right shoulder:

Next row or the Right Side [a Decrease row]—work in pattern to 1 st after marker, slip-slip-knit decrease, k to end—32 (34, 36) sts of Staggered Eyelet pattern and 20 (21, 24) sts of side panel in Stockinette for 52 (55, 60) sts total.

Note: This Decrease row continues outward movement of center panel pattern.

Work a Wrong Side row. Repeat Decrease row—51 (54, 58) sts total, 32 (34, 36) sts of Staggered Eyelet pattern and 19 (20, 22) sts of side panel in Stockinette.

[Repeat Decrease row every 4th row, then every 2nd row alternately] 7 (8, 9) more times, then repeat Decrease row on next Right Side row 1 (0, 0) more time. There are 36 (38, 40) sts at last Decrease row or 32 (34, 36) sts of Staggered Eyelet pattern and 4 sts of side panel in Stockinette.

Work even in patterns until armhole edge measures 7.5 (8, 8.5)" total from the beginning of armhole shaping, end with a Wrong Side row. Bind off.

Sleeves

Cast on 99 (105, 113) sts.

Rib as for back until there are a total of 9 rows, end by finishing a Right Side row. Begin Stockinette st by purling 1 row.

Shape for upper arm:

Next row or the Right Side—k 2, increase, work to within 2 sts from end, increase, k last 2 sts—101 (107, 115) sts.

Continue to increase in this manner every 4th row 3 more times.

Work even on 107 (113, 121) sts until piece measures 3" total from beginning, end ready to work a Right Side row.

Shape for armholes:

Bind off 4 (6, 7) sts at the beginning of the next 2 rows—99 (101, 107) sts.

Next row [a Decrease row], worked on Right Side—k 2, k 2 together, work to within last 4 sts, slip-slip-knit decrease, k last 2 sts—97 (99, 105) sts.

Repeat last Decrease row on next 5 (7, 9) Right Side rows—87 (85, 87) sts. Bind off on next Right Side row.

Finishing

Block pieces to measurements. Sew together top of each front shoulder to top of back. Set in sleeves. Sew side and sleeve seams.

Lily M. Chin

⣿⣿ **A Trio of Shoes:**

Ballet Slippers or Mary Janes, Striped Espadrille, and Ribbed Slide

| Kie Zuraw

CITY: Los Angeles, CA
AGE: 28

Kie taught herself to knit from a book when she was twelve. She's left-handed and did everything in mirror image. This no doubt helped her to be a better knitter, since she really has to "understand" a pattern; she can't just follow the directions word by word. She had been knitting only sweaters from patterns until about two years ago, when she started to feel she needed to go deeper. She got into socks, started reading about different folk traditions, and generally got a lot more adventurous.

Some of her current experiments are reversible textured double-knitting (hard to describe in words—it involves crossing the colors over from one side to the other, with traveling stitches), lace knitting with wire, and fine-gauge knitting that looks like bulky knitting. She has hand-dyed some yarn and is taking a class in drop-spindle spinning. It's been a really exciting and enriching couple of years for her. Kie has always loved knitting, but now she sees that there's so much *more*.

After finishing graduate school at UCLA in 2000, Kie moved across town to USC, where she is now a professor. As a specialist in phonology, she studies how languages organize sounds into patterns. As she puts it, "it's a lot like knitting in some ways, and I'm currently working on a description of knitting patterns using phonological theory for my web page."

Kie grew up mainly in Montreal, but has been living in L.A. for six years now. She's married to a non-knitter named Bryan.

Inspiration

Kie had been speculating about knit shoes. She is six feet tall and has enormous feet (size 11½ or 12). Buying actual women's shoes is almost impossible for her. She wanted to have some fun, pretty, summery shoes of the kind that are worn year-round in L.A.

She had been wondering for a while if there was some way she could make her own shoes. As a vegetarian, she didn't want to work with leather, so that ruled out traditional shoe construction. Knitting was the perfect solution! She can now make leather-free shoes that fit perfectly.

She started with a simple wide band across the front of the foot attached to a pre-made sole (like an open-toe mule). Cotton and viscose/rayon were our yarns of choice for all the shoes. (Try the Drops line of needles from Aurora yarn to prevent slippery stitches. They are made of bamboo and imported from Norway.)

Since the actual knit piece would be so small,

she could try lots of ideas: stripes, lace, floral intarsia. . . . The only hard part about this project would be sewing the top onto the sole. At first Kie thought of using an upholstery needle, but ultimately she settled for the ease of glue.

She also experimented with other shapes: espadrille with strap (mule front with a band that goes around sides and back of foot) and a ballet-type slipper with a button instead of a buckle.

She needed to find a source for pre-made shoe bottoms. Searching around on the Internet turned up nothing that was available retail, so she went to her friendly neighborhood cobbler to ask for advice. He sold her a big sheet of crepe rubber for $24 (enough for several pairs of shoes) and said this would be available from any cobbler. The rubber is easy to cut with an X-acto knife.

Kie's plan was to glue the knitted upper pieces onto the cut-out crepe sole, then glue on a cut-out piece of foam cushion (also from the cobbler), so that the edges of the knit pieces would be sandwiched between sole and cushion. She then glued a nice piece of fabric on top of that. The cobbler recommended that she sand the edges of the sole at some point, and said he could do it for her if she had any trouble.

The results were pretty astounding to me. Instructions are simple enough for beginners. The special materials needed are crepe rubber, foam cushioning material, glue, and fabric. The special tools needed are X-acto knife and sandpaper.

The results so excited us both. Once you get the shoe bottoms, you could make a big wardrobe of shoes for minimal time and money. I love the idea of making shoes to match each and every one of my knit outfits!

▢▢▢▢ Instructions | Ballet Slippers or Mary Janes

Finished Size: Small (Medium, Large), or women's shoe sizes 3–6 (7–9, 10–13).

Size and gauge need only be approximate: when you assemble the shoe, you will be adjusting it to fit your foot exactly.

Materials:

- Aurora/Garnstudio "Cotton Viscose" (54% cotton, 46% viscose, 50g, appx 109yds): 3 skeins #03 Pink.
- Double-pointed knitting needles in size 2 or size to obtain gauge.
- Stitch holder.
- Two 7/8" buttons (ours are from One World Button Supply Co.)
- Piece of 1/4"-thick high-density foam big enough to stand on with both feet—about 13" × 13".
- Piece of crepe rubber, same size.
- Piece of fabric (we used pale green dupione silk), about 36" × 24".
- Rubber cement.
- Aleene's Original Tacky Glue.
- Scissors.
- Several pieces of clean, uninked paper (not newspaper).
- Piece of cardboard, about 8.5" × 11".
- Scotch tape.
- Safety pins.

Gauge: 29 sts and 55 rows = 4" in Garter st [k all rows].

Special Note: Slip-slip-knit is described on page 25.

Left Foot

Toe:

Cast on 34 (42, 50) sts.

Row 1 (Wrong Side)—k 17 (21, 25), place marker, k 17 (21, 25).

K 32 (40, 48) rows.

Next Wrong Side row [a Decrease row]—k to 2 sts before marker, slip-slip-knit decrease, slip marker, knit 2 together to decrease, k to end—32 (40, 48) sts.

Next Right Side row—k across.

Repeat last 2 rows another 2 times, then work the Wrong Side Decrease row again—26 (34, 42) sts.

Next Right Side row [Joining row]—k to marker, remove marker. Fold work in half width-wise, Right Side facing out, so that needles are side by side. Slip 1 st from near needle onto 3rd needle (call this st A), ★slip 1 st from far needle onto 3rd needle (call this st B), pass A over B. Slip 1 st from near needle onto 3rd needle (call this st A), pass B over A. Repeat from ★ until just 1 st remains. Cut yarn, leaving a tail of about 12", and pull end through last st.

Left-hand side:

With Right Side facing you, pick up and k first 12 (15, 18) sts along cast-on edge of toe piece.

K 20 (25, 30) rows, slipping first st of all Wrong Side rows to create a chain-st selvedge.

Continuing in Garter stitch, increase 1 st at outer edge [end of Right Side rows] every 6th row until piece reaches back of heel, about 40 (50, 60) rows total. Cut yarn and put sts on stitch holder.

Right-hand side:

With Right Side facing you, pick up and k last 12 (15, 18) sts along cast-on edge of toe piece.

K 20 (25, 30) rows, slipping first st of all Right Side rows to create chain-st selvedge.

Continuing in Garter stitch, increase 1 st at outer edge [beginning of Right Side rows] every 6th row until piece reaches back of heel, about 40 (50, 60) rows total. Cut yarn, leaving sts on needle.

Join heel:

Transfer sts for left-hand side from holder onto needle and place that needle against the needle with the right-hand-side sts, Right Sides facing out. Use same procedure as for toe to bind off together: Slip st (A) from near needle onto 3rd needle, ★slip st (B) from far needle onto 3rd needle, pass A over B. Slip st (A) from near needle onto 3rd needle, pass B over A. Repeat from ★ until just one st remains. Pass end of yarn through last st.

With the length of yarn left from joining the toe, very loosely sew the undersides of the toe together, and the bottom edge of the right-hand side to the bottom edge of the left-hand side. Sew in a loose zigzag so that the edges don't even touch. This will allow you to adjust the size of the shoe.

Strap:

Pick up and k 4 sts from middle of right-hand side. Make I-cord as follows: k across, then without turning, slide sts back and k across again with same side facing you. Continue until cord reaches left-hand side when shoe is on foot, then k another 2". Bind off and sew end of cord to a point ½" before end of cord to form a loop the right size for your buttons.

Right Foot

Work as for left foot, but pick up sts for strap on left-hand side.

Assembly

Trace a favorite sandal onto a piece of cardboard and cut out the shape. Try slipping the insole into the knit shoe and standing in it to see if you want to make any adjustments.

Trace the cardboard sole shape onto the ¼" foam, then flip the shape over and trace again for the other foot. Cut out the two foam insoles, exactly along the lines. Place the insoles on clean paper and cover the top surfaces with rubber cement.

Use your cardboard sole to cut two pieces of fabric shaped like the insoles but about 1" bigger all around. Place the fabric pieces on clean paper and cover with rubber cement.

When the insoles and fabric are dry (about 2 hours), place each insole upside down on the corresponding piece of fabric, so that the rubber-cemented surfaces of foam and fabric are in contact. Turn the insole and attached fabric over and rub out any air bubbles using scissor handles.

Flip the insoles, now glued to fabric, upside down again. Cut several slits in the edge of the fabric, perpendicular to the edge of the foam (so that it will be easier to wrap the fabric edges around the underside of the foam). Cover the outer ½" of the foam with rubber cement and allow to dry. Then carefully fold the edge of the fabric onto the underside of the foam and smooth with scissor handles. Cut off any excess fabric.

Now trace the cardboard sole shape onto the crepe rubber, then flip the shape over and trace again for the other foot. Cut out these two bottom soles, exactly along the lines you drew.

You now have a pair of insoles, their top surfaces covered in fabric, and a pair of bottom soles. You will now determine how tightly to stretch the knit uppers. Place the insoles inside the shoes, using safety pins to secure the straps. Adjust the loose zigzag sewing on the undersides of the shoes. Temporarily secure the undersides of the shoes with Scotch tape and walk around, continuing to adjust.

When you are satisfied with how the knit piece fits, secure the loose end of the sewing on the underside. Remove the Scotch tape and, without disturbing the placement of the insole too much, cover the underside of the insole with tacky glue, avoiding getting glue too close to the edges. Get the glue well in under the knitting to secure it to the insole. Coat the knitting with tacky glue also, to saturate it.

Carefully place the insole-and-knitting on top of the crepe rubber sole. Weight the shoe down with heavy books and let dry overnight.

When the shoes are dry, try them on and adjust the safety pins to determine the best placement for a button. Then sew a button to the outer side of each shoe.

Instructions | Striped Espadrille

Finished Size: Small (Medium, Large), or women's shoe sizes 3–6 (7–9, 10–13).

Size and gauge need only be approximate: when you assemble the shoe, you will be adjusting it to fit your foot exactly.

Materials:

- Aurora/Garnstudio "Muskat" (100% Egyptian cotton, 50g, appx 109yds): 1 skein each color #51 Light Orange (color B) #53 Light Green (Color C), #47 Bright Orange (color D), and #30 Pale Yellow (color E); plus 2 skeins color #44 Dark Green (color A).
- Size 2 knitting needles, or size needed to obtain gauge.
- Size 2 double-pointed knitting needles, or same size as above.
- Piece of 1/4"-thick high-density foam big enough to stand on with both feet—about 13" × 13".
- Piece of 1"-thick high-density foam, same size.
- Piece of crepe rubber, same size.
- Piece of fabric (we used pale green dupione silk), about 36" × 24".
- Rubber cement.
- Tacky glue.
- Scissors.
- Sharp knife.
- Several pieces of clean, uninked paper (not newspaper).
- Piece of cardboard, about 8.5" × 11".
- Scotch tape.
- Rubber bands.
- Pencil.

Gauge: 28 sts and 39 rows = 4" in Stockinette st [k on Right Side rows, p on Wrong Side rows]. Fabric should be very tight.

Abbreviations:

Gst = Garter stitch [k all Right Side rows, k all Wrong Side rows]

Sst = Stockinette stitch [k all Right Side rows, p all Wrong Side rows]

Left Foot

Cast on 45 (50, 60) sts with A.

Work 0 (2, 4) rows of Gst with A.

Work 2 rows of Sst with A.

Work 3 rows of Sst with B.

Work 5 rows of Sst with C.

Work 1 row of Sst with D.

Work 8 rows of Sst with E.

Work 3 (3, 5) rows of Sst with B.

Work 0 (4, 4) rows of Sst with C.

Work 1 row of Sst with A.

Work 2 rows of Sst with D.

Work 0 (0, 1) row of Sst with E.

Work 0 (0, 1) row of Sst with C.

Work 0 (0, 2) rows of Sst with A.

Work 4 rows of Gst with A.

Bind off.

Right Foot

Same as for left foot.

Assembly

Trace a favorite sandal onto a piece of cardboard and cut out the shape. Try standing on the shape, or slipping the shape into the top of the sandal to see if you want to make any adjustments.

Trace the cardboard sole shape onto the ¼" foam, then flip the shape over and trace again for the other foot. Cut out the two foam insoles, staying ¼" inside the lines. Place the insoles on clean paper and cover the top surfaces with rubber cement.

Use your cardboard sole to cut out two pieces of fabric shaped like the insoles but about 1" bigger all around. Place the fabric pieces on clean paper and cover with rubber cement.

When the insoles and fabric are dry (about 2 hours), place each insole upside down on the corresponding piece of fabric, so that the rubber-cemented surfaces of foam and fabric are in contact. Turn the insole and attached fabric over and rub out any air bubbles using scissor handles.

Flip the insoles, now glued to fabric, upside down again. Cut several slits in the edge of the fabric, perpendicular to the edge of the foam (so that it will be easier to wrap the fabric edges around the underside of the foam). Cover the outer ½" of the foam with rubber cement and allow to dry. Then carefully fold the edge of the fabric onto the underside of the foam and smooth with scissor handles. Cut off any excess fabric.

Now trace the cardboard sole shape onto the 1" foam, then flip it over and trace again for the other foot. Cut out the two foam midsoles, exactly along the lines you drew. Cut two strips of fabric each long enough to go all the way around the edge of the midsoles, and 1¾" wide. Place the midsoles on clean paper, and cover the edges and the outer ½" of the top surfaces with rubber cement. Place the fabric strips on clean paper and cover with rubber cement.

When the rubber cement is dry, place the fabric strips around the edges of the midsoles and smooth out. There should be ⅜" of the fabric strip extending below and above the foam. Cut slits all around the upper extra fabric and smooth it onto the top surface of the foam, cutting off excess fabric if necessary. Flip the midsoles over and cover the outer ½" of the underside of the midsoles with rubber cement. Let the rubber cement dry. Cut slits all around the excess fabric, smoothing it onto the foam, and cutting off excess fabric.

You now have a pair of insoles, their top surfaces covered in fabric, and a pair of midsoles, their outer edges covered in fabric. You will now determine how tightly to stretch the knit uppers. Place the knit piece across the insole so that the cast-on and bound-off edges run across it. Put the left and right edges of the knit piece under the insole so that the knit piece feels snug. Temporarily attach the knit piece with Scotch tape. Now use rubber bands to temporarily attach the insole to the midsole. Do the same to the other shoe. Walk around a bit and adjust the knit piece until it feels very snug but not uncomfortable.

When you are satisfied with the placement of the knit piece, use a pencil to lightly trace the left and right edges of the knit piece onto the midsole, working your pencil in under the insole so

that the line is ¼" in from the edge of the insole.

Take off the insole, and use a knife to cut through the midsole where you have marked in pencil. You now have a slit on either side of the midsole that will be covered by the insole.

Now push the left and right edges of the knit piece through the slits in the midsole, and replace the insole. Temporarily tape the edges of the knit piece under the midsole and walk around, adjusting the tightness of the knit pieces.

When you are satisfied, use extra yarn (or ends from the piece if they haven't been worked in yet) to sew the sides of the knit piece together under the midsole. The sides won't actually touch, but the sewing will help keep them at the right tension. Walk around once more to make sure it's right and then take off the rubber bands.

Trace your cardboard sole shape onto the crepe rubber, and flip the shape over to trace again for the other foot. Cut out the two bottom soles. Cover the bottom surface of the midsole with tacky glue, making sure to saturate the yarn there. Don't place any glue too close to the edges or it will seep out.

Carefully place the midsole onto the corresponding crepe rubber bottom sole. Cover the bottom of the insole with tacky glue and carefully slide it under the knit piece and onto the midsole.

Place rubber bands around the toe and heel and near the edges of the knit piece to ensure good contact between insole and midsole. Place some heavy books on top of the shoes and let the glue dry overnight.

Heel strap and piping:

Pick up 5 sts from the left end of the cast-on edge of the toe piece. Work in k 1, p 1 Ribbing every row until the strap is long enough to reach around your heel. Try the shoe on to make sure the strap is snug enough, then bind off and sew the strap to the right end of the toe piece. Repeat for the other foot.

Make I-cord to decorate insole-midsole juncture:

With double-pointed needles, cast on 3 sts.

★K across. Without turning work, slide the yarn to the other end of the needle and repeat from ★.

Continue until cord reaches from insole-midsole juncture at left top of toe piece, around toe of shoe, to right top of toe piece, and cast off.

Make another I-cord long enough to reach from left bottom of toe piece, around heel of shoe, to right bottom of toe piece. Repeat for the other foot.

Place a thin line of tacky glue on the insole-midsole juncture, skipping the knit toe piece, and attach the I-cords. Let dry overnight.

◫◫◫◫ Instructions | Ribbed Slide

Finished Size: Small (Medium, Large), or women's shoe sizes 3–6 (7–9, 10–13).

Size and gauge need only be approximate: when you assemble the shoe, you will be adjusting it to fit your foot exactly.

Materials:

- Aurora/Garnstudio "Muskat" (100% Egyptian cotton, 50g, appx 109yds): 2 skeins #04 Lavender.
- Size 2 knitting needles, or size needed to obtain gauge.
- Piece of 1/4"-thick high-density foam big enough to stand on with both feet—about 13" × 13".
- Piece of 1/2"-thick high-density foam, same size.
- Piece of crepe rubber, same size.
- Piece of fabric (we used pale green dupione silk), about 36" × 24".
- Rubber cement.
- Tacky glue.
- Scissors.
- Sharp knife.
- Several pieces of clean, uninked paper (not newspaper).
- Piece of cardboard, about 8.5" × 11".
- Scotch tape.
- Rubber bands.
- Pencil.

Gauge: 38 sts and 32 rows = 4" in pattern stitch.

Special Note: Slip-slip-knit is described on page 25.

Abbreviations:

Rib = on Wrong Side rows, k the k sts and p the p sts; on Right Side rows, k the k sts [*but* k them through their back loops and p the p sts].

Left Foot

Cast on 44 (52, 60) sts.

Row 1 [Wrong Side]—[k 1, p 1] 11 (13, 15) times, k 1, place st marker, p 1, [k 1, p 1] to end.

Row 2 and all Right Side rows—Rib to marker, k 2 together to decrease, Rib to end.

Row 3 and all Wrong Side rows—Rib.

Repeat Rows 2 and 3 until no sts remain before marker, then bind off.

Right Foot

Cast on 44 (52, 60) sts.

Row 1 [Wrong Side]—[k 1, p 1] 12 (14, 16) times, place st marker, [k 1, p 1] to end.

Row 2 and all Right Side rows—Rib to marker, slip-slip-knit decrease, rib to end.

Row 3 and all Wrong Side rows—Rib.

Work until no sts remain before marker, then bind off.

Assembly

Trace a favorite sandal onto a piece of cardboard and cut out the shape. Try standing on the shape, or slipping the shape into the top of the sandal to see if you want to make any adjustments.

Trace the cardboard sole shape onto the 1/4" foam, then flip the shape over and trace again for the other foot. Cut out the two foam insoles, staying 1/4" inside the lines. Place the insoles on clean paper and cover the top surfaces with rubber cement.

Use your cardboard sole to cut out two pieces of fabric shaped like the insoles but about 1" bigger all around. Place the fabric pieces on clean paper and cover with rubber cement.

When the insoles and fabric are dry (about 2 hours), place each insole upside down on the corresponding piece of fabric, so that the rubber-cemented surfaces of foam and fabric are in contact. Turn the insole and attached fabric over and rub out any air bubbles using scissor handles.

Flip the insoles, now glued to fabric, upside down again. Cut several slits in the edge of the fabric, perpendicular to the edge of the foam (so that it will be easier to wrap the fabric edges around the underside of the foam). Cover the outer 1/2" of the foam with rubber cement and allow to dry. Then carefully fold the edge of the fabric onto the underside of the foam and smooth with scissor handles. Cut off any excess fabric.

Now trace the cardboard sole shape onto the 1/2" foam, then flip the shape over and trace again for the other foot. Cut out the two foam midsoles, exactly along the lines you drew. Cut two strips of fabric each long enough to go all the way around the edge of the midsoles, and 1 3/4" wide. Place the midsoles on clean paper, and cover the edges and the outer ½" of the top surfaces with rubber cement. Place the fabric strips on clean paper and cover with rubber cement.

When the rubber cement is dry, place the fabric strips around the edges of the midsoles and smooth out. There should be about ⅜" of the fabric strip extending below and above the foam. Cut slits all around the upper extra fabric and smooth it onto the top surface of the foam, cutting off excess fabric if necessary. Flip the midsoles over and cover the outer ½" of the underside of the midsoles with rubber cement. Let the rubber cement dry, cut slits all around the excess fabric, smooth it onto the foam, and cut off excess fabric.

You now have a pair of insoles, their top surfaces covered in fabric, and a pair of midsoles, their outer edges covered in fabric. You will now determine how tightly to stretch the knit uppers. Place the knit piece across the insole so that the cast-on and bound-off edges run across it, with the cast-on edge at the inside edge of your foot, so that the knit piece is wider over the knuckle of your big toe than at your pinkie toe. Put the left and right edges of the knit piece under the insole so that the knit piece feels snug.

Temporarily attach the knit piece with Scotch tape. Now use rubber bands to temporarily attach the insole to the midsole. Do the same to the other

shoe. Walk around a bit and adjust the knit piece until it feels very snug but not uncomfortable.

When you are satisfied with the placement of the knit piece, use a pencil to lightly trace the left and right edges of the knit piece onto the midsole, working your pencil in under the insole so that the line is ¼" in from the edge of the insole.

Take off the insole, and use a knife to cut through the midsole where you have marked in pencil. You now have a slit on either side of the midsole that will be covered by the insole.

Now push the left and right edges of the knit piece through the slits in the midsole, and replace the insole. Temporarily tape the edges of the knit piece under the midsole and walk around, adjusting the tightness of the knit pieces.

When you are satisfied, use extra yarn (or ends from the piece if they haven't been worked in yet) to sew the sides of the knit piece together under the midsole. The sides won't actually touch, but the sewing will help keep them at the right tension. Walk around once more to make sure it's right and then take off the rubber bands.

Trace your cardboard sole shape onto the crepe rubber, and flip the shape over to trace again for the other foot. Cut out the two bottom soles. Cover the bottom surface of the midsole with tacky glue, making sure to saturate the yarn there.

Don't place any glue too close to the edges or it will seep out.

Carefully place the midsole onto the corresponding crepe rubber bottom sole. Cover the bottom of the insole with tacky glue and carefully slide it under the knit piece and onto the midsole.

Place rubber bands around the toe and heel and near the edges of the knit piece to ensure good contact between insole and midsole. Place some heavy books on top of the shoes and let the glue dry overnight.

A Slew of Socks | Catherine Schroeder

CITY: Cleveland, OH
AGE: 23

Catherine lives in Cleveland, a couple of blocks away from the Case Western Reserve University campus, where she went to college. She grew up just outside Washington, D.C., and got started in fiber stuff right after her twelfth birthday.

Catherine soon grew tired of the counted cross-stitch kits she had and decided to move on to other things. One of her aunts helped her pick out a nice crochet sweater pattern and enough yarn to do it. Her mother taught her the basic stitches. Ultimately Catherine made a different sweater from the one she intended, and although it looked pretty good for a first sweater, she felt it was not quite fashionable enough for someone just finishing seventh grade.

She continued to crochet for a while, until she got to college and realized that there were a whole lot more resources for knitting. So during her freshman year, she bought a random pair of knitting needles (10" size 4 single points) and a really poorly written booklet that taught the absolute basics of knitting. Eventually she worked it out herself. (She knows she purls backwards, but it always turns out just right in the end.)

Catherine discovered better fiber sources from a knitter she met on the D.C. Metro in 1997. Armed with good yarn, she then went a little bit over the edge. Her "not currently earmarked for some project" yarn stash is over thirty balls! She won't mention that she's working on at least seven projects plus another four or five that are just in her head, waiting to be realized. She started to get bored with most printed patterns, and not long ago started designing her own stuff. She still uses patterns, but mostly as a reference for things she can't do.

As you can see Catherine is mostly self-taught from craft-store books. Nowadays she does a lot of messing around with designing her own things, some with better results than others. She actually prefers modifying existing structures, since she knows that they will hang right, but still have her own distinctive look.

Inspiration

Catherine liked the idea of doing several small projects, and socks were a favorite. She says, "I am somewhat of a sockster. My cousins (six kids between two and fourteen) got socks and/or hats for Christmas last year and I keep on making socks. Any sweater that has enough leftover yarn gets matching socks." She opted to do a whole slew of socks in all different styles. That way, each sock could showcase a different stitch or technique. We wanted to include Fair Isle or stranded colorwork, Mosaic-type knitting with slip-stitches, a simple rib, a basic sock. . . . Socks are a great way to try out new things without the commitment of a whole garment.

Of course, this requires practice with the use of double-pointed needles, or dpns. Many knitters fear them. The initial juggling of a set of four or five needles seems daunting. Fear not, you are using only two at a time and the others are in holding-position. Most knitters cast on all the stitches required onto one needle first, then separate them evenly onto the other dpns thereafter.

Socks also offer plenty of opportunities to knit in public (or *kip,* as it is referred to in Internet knitting communities). They are small and portable. If done with a thicker yarn on larger needles in a bigger gauge, they become Christmas stockings.

The incredible range of sock yarns we chose covers the spectrum of what's in the market today. There are blends of wool/nylon, wool/cotton/nylon, cotton/nylon. Although any thin yarn may be used for socks, the nylon content helps them hold up better. Nylon gives strength and reinforcement. Catherine was especially enamored of the cottons because they are seasonless.

I left Catherine mostly to her own devices. She came up with a formula so that all the socks follow the same basic set of directions (leg, heel, foot, toe). The number of stitches varies with size. The only real difference is the pattern used on the leg and foot, and the colors. So there is one set of instructions for all of them.

The short-rowed heel is one of the easier heels to master. The ability to turn the heel on a sock is a sign of an accomplished knitter. When working the color patterns of Fair Isle or Mosaic in the round, the beginnings of the rows will seem "off." This is known as a color jog, and it represents the juncture where the ends of the rows meet with the beginnings of the next rows. This is normal and not a cause for concern.

Catherine designed many of these socks "on the needle" as she knitted. She says, "When I design anything, be it socks (most often) or sweaters (total of four times), I map out a general plan, and pick out colors and a pattern to start with. When I get close to another decision point I put down my work and plan some more, taking what I've done into consideration. And so it goes. It's almost meditative for me to think and plan as I knit, letting the project knit itself as it goes."

With the Plain socks in a 2 × 2 Ribbing, the excitement comes from the yarn itself, which looks vaguely cowlike! Fair Isle socks look more complex than they really are. Although there are three colors, only two are worked on any given row. The cute little Athletic shorty socks are loosely modeled after commercial Thor-Lo® socks; heel and toe in contrasting grayish blue add pizzazz. Note how the Mosaic socks are Garter stitch–based at the leg and top, yet smooth Stockinette at the foot's bottom is used for comfort. These are thicker and work as house socks or may be worn with boots or sandals.

Catherine had the most problems with the variegated yarn. The colors are stunning, but it was hard to find a stitch pattern that would have enough inherent stretch for the cotton (which has very little elasticity), and still show off the variegation.

She swatched some early ideas, the first of which made the variegation stand out well, but was far too dense and not stretchy enough. That's when I suggested a signature technique of mine, reversible cables. It is a 2 × 2 Ribbing base where mini 2-stitch cables make up the rib in both the knit as well as the purl sections. It also creates a reversible cabled fabric—so cuffs can be turned down as well!

Catherine thought it very gorgeous, but the inelastic nature of the matte cotton made it slow-going because she had to go down to a very small needle size to get it to be a little stretchier.

However, using the Addi Turbo® double-pointed needles eased this quite a lot. The yarn is a matte cotton so the slippery needles prevented "drag." The sleekness of the needles makes for faster knitting in general, except perhaps when working with equally slippery yarn.

Instructions | A Slew of Socks

Finished Sizes: Child (Small Woman, Average Woman, Large Woman/Average Man, Large Man).

Materials:

A. Plain 2 × 2 Rib: Skacel/Schoeller Esslinger "Fortissima Colori" (75% wool, 25% nylon, 50 g, appx 210m/228yds): 1 (1,2,2,2) skeins #459 Spotted Cow Print.

B. Fair Isle: Skacel/Schoeller Esslinger "Fortissima Cottolana" (38% wool, 37% cotton, 25% nylon, 50g, appx 210m/228yds): 1 skein each #11 Tan, #06 Brown, and #14 Charcoal.

C. Variegated Reversible Cables: Skacel/Schoeller Esslinger "Fortissima Cotton Colori" (75% cotton, 25% nylon, 50g, appx 210m/228yds): 1 (2, 2, 2, 2) skeins #04 Fuchsia/Blue/Green Multi.

D. Athletic Shorty: Skacel/Schoeller Esslinger "Fortissima Cotton" (75% cotton, 25% nylon, 50g, appx 210m/228yds): 1 (1, 1, 2, 2) skeins #01 White, 1 skein #61 Light Blue.

E. Mosaic: Skacel/Schoeller Esslinger "Fortissima" (75% wool, 25% nylon, 50g, appx 210m/228yds): 1 (2, 2, 2, 2) skeins #06 Deep Red, 1 skein #184 Nearly Black.

F. All Socks: Double-pointed knitting needles (we used Skacel/Addi "Turbo"®) in size 1 for legs and size 0 for heels and toes. Or use whatever size it takes to get the gauge.

Gauge: 32 sts = 4" in Stockinette st and in Mosaic pattern for all socks except for the Fair Isle, which yielded 36 sts = 4".

Note, however, that gauge isn't crucial on this project. Socks tend to be stretchy. Since these are small projects, if you find a sock is coming out larger or smaller than desired, change needle size accordingly to make it smaller or larger.

Special Notes: Directions for heel and toe are the same for all socks. All sock constructions are the same; what changes are patterns used. Also note that sock E, the Mosaic, can only be done in Child, Average Woman, and Large Man, due to the number of repeats. Always slip sts as if to purl, or in a purlwise fashion, so as not to twist them.

Slip-slip-knit = [slip next st as if to knit] twice, insert the left-hand needle from left to right through the fronts of these 2 sts, then knit the two together in this position [through their back loops].

Patterns

A. 2 × 2 Ribbing: [k 2, p 2] around. K the knit sts and p the purl sts on each subsequent round or row.

B. Fair Isle: Follow pattern chart [a 12-st and 10-row repeat], reading chart from right to left at all times since work is knit circularly [in the round]. All sts are knit with Right Side facing you; just work the st in the color presented in the chart.

C. Reversible Cables:

Front twist: Knit the 2nd stitch on the left needle. Don't take the stitch off the needle. Knit the first stitch. Take both stitches off.

Back twist: Same as for front twist but worked in purl instead of knit.

Row 1—[front twist, p 2] around.

Row 2—[k 2, back twist] around.

Repeat Rows 1 and 2.

E. Mosaic: Follow pattern chart [a 24 st and 10-row repeat], reading chart from right to left at all times since work is knit circularly [in the round].

Each chart row represents *two* rows of knitting. That is, work each chart row twice. When working the row a second time, follow chart again and *purl* the sts instead of knitting for Garter Mosaic. If the repeat row is knitted again, Stockinette Mosaic is formed and is used for the bottom of the foot.

You will only be working with one yarn on any given row. When the row calls for that color and the chart indicates the other color, *slip* that st as if to purl with the yarn in the back.

For All Socks

Cast on 48 (60, 72, 84, 96) sts with color noted below. Arrange on 3 double-pointed needles, or dpns, so that there are 16 (20, 24, 28, 32) stitches on each dpn.

Leg

Sock A: [k 2, p 2] around. Repeat this for 4–8". Ours measure 6.5". Before you begin the heel, knit only 1 st onto the end of the last row so that the rib pattern lines up evenly on the foot and looks symmetrical.

Sock B: Cast on with tan. [k 2, p 2] around. Repeat this for 12 rows total. Begin Fair Isle color chart in Stockinette [k all rounds] with 4 (5, 6, 7, 8) repeats around. Work 50 rows, or 5 vertical repeats of the chart. Begin heel by working Row 1 of the chart over first dpn, then switch to unpatterned Stockinette thereafter in tan. Brown needs to be at this end for later use.

Sock C: [k 2, p 2] around. Repeat this for 12

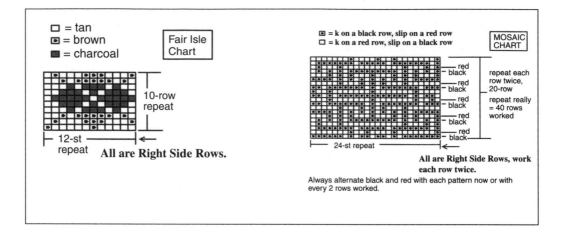

Fair Isle Chart

10-row repeat

12-st repeat **All are Right Side Rows.**

◙ = k on a black row, slip on a red row
□ = k on a red row, slip on a black row

MOSAIC CHART

red
black
red
black
red
black
red
black
red
black
red
black

repeat each row twice, 20-row

repeat really = 40 rows worked

24-st repeat

All are Right Side Rows, work each row twice.

Always alternate black and red with each pattern now or with every 2 rows worked.

rows total. Begin Reversible Cables pattern and work until the sock is 5.75" or desired length to heel.

Sock D: Cast on with white.

Row 1—p around.

Row 2 and *all even rows*—[slip 1, k 1] around.

Rows 3 and 5—p around.

Row 7—k around.

Repeat Rows 6 and 7 until cuff measures 2". End on an odd row. Knit 5 rows Join blue and work heel in blue.

Sock E: Cast on with red. [k 1, p 1] around for 12 rows total. Begin Mosaic color chart with 2 (0, 3, 0, 4) repeats around. Work for 120 rows, or 3 vertical repeats of the chart [20 chart rows]. Work both parts of the first row again. Work heel in red.

Short Row Heel

Arrange the stitches so that there are 24 (30, 36, 42, 48) sts on first dpn, 12 (15, 18, 21, 24) sts on second dpn, and 12 (15, 18, 21, 24) sts on third dpn. The heel is worked back and forth on the first dpn.

With the heel color, k across to within the last st of first dpn [sock B is worked in pattern]. Keep yarn in back, slip the last st to the right-hand dpn as if to p, bring yarn to the front, slip last st back onto left-hand dpn. Turn work.

Bring yarn to the front [yarn is now fully wrapped around the slipped st], p to within last st. Keep yarn in front, slip last st, bring yarn to the back, slip last st back onto left-hand dpn. Turn work.

Bring yarn to the back [yarn is now fully wrapped around the slipped st], k to st before previous slipped st—2 sts on left-hand needle. Slip next st with yarn in back, bring yarn to the front, place slipped st from right-hand dpn back onto left-hand dpn. Turn work.

★Bring yarn to the front [yarn is now fully wrapped around the slipped st], p to st before previous slipped st. Keep yarn in front, slip next st, bring yarn to the back, place slipped st from right-hand dpn back onto left-hand dpn. Turn work.

Bring yarn to the back [yarn is now fully wrapped around the slipped st], k to st before previous slipped st. Slip next st with yarn in back, bring yarn to the front, place slipped st from right-hand dpn back onto left-hand dpn. Turn work.

Repeat from ★. There will be 1 less st worked with each "short row." Work until p 8 (10, 12, 14, 16) has been completed. Wrap and turn as before.

Next row—bring yarn to the back, k 8 (10, 12, 14, 16) or to within next wrapped st. Insert right-hand dpn into front of wrap from bottom to top as if to k, then insert right-hand dpn into st itself also as if to k, k both the wrap and st together [it's a little tricky but wangle the new loop through]. Repeat this across the remainder of the dpn.

Using first dpn as right-hand dpn, slip first st of second dpn with yarn in back, bring yarn to the front, place slipped st from right-hand dpn back onto left-hand dpn or second dpn. Turn work.

Go back to using fourth dpn as right-hand dpn. Give yarn a tug to tighten, p across first dpn sts to within next wrapped st.

With right-hand dpn, pick up wrap from behind and place wrap fully [up and over] onto left-hand dpn—it looks like there are 2 sts on the needle. P both the wrap and the st together. Repeat this across the remainder of the dpn.

Continue using same right-hand dpn and slip first st of third dpn with yarn in front, bring yarn to the back, place slipped st from right-hand dpn back onto left-hand dpn or third dpn. Turn work.

Go back to using fourth dpn as right-hand dpn. Give yarn a tug to tighten, k 16 (20, 24, 28, 32) across first dpn, slip next st, bring yarn to front, place slipped st from right-hand dpn back onto left-hand dpn. Turn work. Bring yarn to the front and p 8 (10, 12, 14, 16), slip next st, bring yarn to the back, place slipped st from right-hand dpn back onto left-hand dpn. Turn work.

★K to within wrapped st, k st together with wrap as before, wrap next st as before, turn work. P to within wrapped st, p st together with wrap as before, wrap next st as before, turn work. Repeat from ★ until last st on p row has been wrapped.

K across all sts on first dpn, closing up wrap at last st. Closing up wrap at first st of second dpn and the last st of third dpn, work across the next two dpns in pattern established from the leg (A = k 2, p 2 Ribbing; B = pattern Row 1; C = pattern Row 1 or 2; D = change to white; E = pattern Row 2). Don't forget to close up the wrap on the first st of first dpn when continuing in pattern hereafter.

Foot

Sock A. Work Stockinette st [k all rounds] over all sts that were heel sts (they are now bottom-of-the-foot sts), [k 2, p 2] Ribbing over top-of-the-foot sts. Continue until about 2" shorter than foot. Try on, piece should be at small toe.

Sock B. Continue pattern all around [begin Row 2 of pattern], including bottom of the foot. Work until about 2" shorter than foot. Try on, piece should be at small toe.

Sock C. Work Stockinette st [k all rounds] over all sts that were heel sts (they are now bottom-of-the-foot sts), work Reversible Cables pattern over top-of-the-foot sts. Continue until about 2" shorter than foot. Try on, piece should be at small toe.

Sock D. Cut blue. Continue with white and k around until about 2" shorter than foot. Try on, piece should be at small toe.

Sock E. Continue pattern [second part of Row 2 of pattern] *but,* for bottom-of-foot (which were formerly heel) sts, knit every row rather than purling every other row. This will look a little strange, but will be so much more comfortable to walk on. Continue until about 2" shorter than foot. Try on, piece should be at small toe.

Toe

Change to toe color if necessary [B = tan; D = blue, E = red]. For B, D, and E, end off all other colors not used. Knit across first and second dpns. Third dpn is now beginning of the row and will be deemed first dpn from now on.

Row 1—first dpn: k to within last 3 sts, k 2 together to decrease, k 1; second dpn: k 1, slip-slip-knit to decrease, k to within last 3 sts, k 2 together to decrease, k 1; third dpn: k 1, slip-slip-knit to decrease, k 1.

Row 2—k around.

Repeat Rows 1 and 2 until 16 (20, 24, 28, 32) sts remain, ending with a Row 1. K 4 (5, 6, 7, 8) sts from first dpn onto third dpn. Graft toes together (Elizabeth Zimmermann has super instructions for this in *Knitting Without Tears*) by leaving a long 16" tail. Thread tail through tapestry needle and weave back and forth from front and back pieces, mimicking the stitches. An alternative is to turn sock inside out and work 3-needle bind-off (see page 87).

Hide all of your ends. Block anything that doesn't lie nicely. Don't block the Garter parts of the Mosaic sock, or the Ribbing parts, or the mini-cable parts of the cotton sock. The Fair Isle one will probably need lots of blocking, unless you're super-expert at Fair Isle on three needles, and even then it's not a bad idea.

Suppliers

AURORA YARNS
2385 Carlos St.
P.O. Box 3068
Moss Beach, CA 94038
(650) 728-2730
FAX (650) 728-8539
aurorayarns@pacbell.net

BROWN SHEEP COMPANY
100662 Country Rd. 16
Mitchell, NE 69357-2136
(800) 826-9136
FAX (308) 635-2198
www.brownsheep.com

BRYSON DISTRIBUTING
4065 W. 11th Ave. #39
Eugene, OR 97402-5616
(800) 544-8992

FAX (541) 334-6489
www.brysonknits.com

CARON INTERNATIONAL
P.O. Box 222
Washington, NC 27889
FAX (252) 975-7309
www.caron.com

CASCADE YARNS
2401 Utah Ave. S.
Seattle, WA 98134-1436
(800) 548-1048
FAX (206) 628-2975
sales@cascadeyarninc.com
www.cascadeyarns.com

CHERRY TREE HILL YARN
52 Church St.

P.O. Box 659
Barton, VT 05822
(802) 525-3311
FAX (802) 525-3336
cheryl@cherryyarn.com
www.cherryyarn.com

CLASSIC ELITE YARNS
300A Jackson St.
Lowell, MA 01852
(800) 343-0308
FAX (978) 452-3085
classicelite@aol.com

JUDI & CO.
Judy Alweil, Proprietor
18 Gallatin Dr.
Dix Hills, NY 11746
(631) 499-8480

FAX (631) 462-5290
judicol@attglobal.net

K1C2 SOLUTIONS!
2220 Eastman Ave. #11
Ventura, CA 93003
(800) 607-2462
FAX (805) 676-1175
k1c2@ix.netcom.com

KARABELLA YARNS
1201 Broadway
New York, NY 10001
(212) 679-3516
FAX (646) 935-0588
www.schoolproducts.com/yarn/

LION BRAND YARNS
34 W. 15th St.
New York, NY 10011
(212) 243-8995
FAX (212) 627-8154
www.lionbrand.com

MUENCH YARNS
285 Bel Marin Keys Blvd.
Novato, CA 94949
(415) 883-6375

FAX (415) 883-6277
muenchyarn@aol.com

NATURALLY YARNS
S. R. Kertzer Limited
105A Winges Rd.
Woodbridge, ONT L4L 6C2
CANADA
(800) 263-2354
FAX (905) 856-5585
info@kertzer.com
www.kertzer.com

ONE WORLD BUTTON
  SUPPLY CO.
41 Union Square W., Rm. 311
New York, NY 10003
(212) 691-1331
FAX (212) 691-1331
sm1world@idt.net

PATONS
320 Livingston Ave. S.
Listowel, ONT N4W 3H3
CANADA
(800) 265-2864
FAX (519) 291-3232
www.patonsyarn.com

PRYM WILLIAM
400 Hartford Pike
Killingly (Dayville), CT 06241

SKACEL COLLECTION
P.O. Box 88110
Seattle, WA 98138-2110
(253) 854-2710
FAX (253) 854-2571
www.skacelknitting.com

TRENDSETTER YARNS
16742 Stagg St. Ste. 104
Van Nuys, CA 91406
(800) 446-2425
FAX (818) 780-5498
Trndstr@aol.com

WESTMINISTER FIBERS
5 Northern Blvd., Ste. 3
Amherst, NH 03031-2335
(800) 445-9276
FAX (603) 886-1056
wfibers@aol.com

Resources

There is nothing like visiting a good yarn shop to find someone to hold your hand and guide you through knitting's finer points. Unfortunately, not everyone has one nearby; fortunately, there are many avenues to gaining knowledge, finding support, and getting answers to questions.

Online

The Internet is one of the quickest ways to get a response to a query or dilemma. Thousands of knitters worldwide communicate with each other online via "mailing lists," "bulletin boards," and "chat rooms." Here are a few useful sites. Do a web search to find more updated information.

www.woolworks.org
A resources page to other lists, includes free patterns and links.

www.knitting.about.com
A compendium of knitting information from a variety of sources.

groups.yahoo.com/group/knitlist
Subscribe to this mailing list, which has more than 2,700 members.

www.knittinguniverse.com/nav.taf?Page=knitu/index.taf&ButtonSet=community
Owned by *Knitter's* magazine, this mailing list boasts over 4,700 members.

www.Knitnet.com
An online magazine, published quarterly.

Magazines

These periodicals keep readers up-to-date on the latest news, trends, fashions, and patterns.

FAMILY CIRCLE EASY KNITTING PLUS
  CROCHET
233 Spring St.
New York, NY 10013
www.fceasyknitting.com

INTERWEAVE KNITS
201 E. 4th St.
Loveland, CO 80537
(800) 272-2193
hollyd@interweave.com

KNIT 'N STYLE
234 Newton-Sparta Rd.
Newton, NJ 07860
(973) 383-8080
www.knitnstyle.com

KNITTER'S
231 South Phillips Ave., Ste. 400
Sioux Falls, SD 57104
(800) 722-2558
FAX (605) 338-2994
www.knittinguniverse.com

VOGUE KNITTING INTERNATIONAL
233 Spring St.
New York, NY 10013
www.vogueknitting.com

Books

Bliss, Debbie. *How to Knit: The Definitive Knitting Course Complete with Step-by-Step Techniques, Stitch Library and Projects for Your Home and Family.* London: Trafalgar Square, 1999.

Buss, Katharina. *Big Book of Knitting.* New York: Sterling Publications, 1999.

Diven, Gail, Cindy Kitchel, (Introduction), and Nancy Lindemeyer. *The Complete Idiot's Guide to Knitting and Crocheting.* London: Alpha Books, 1999.

Editors of *Vogue. Vogue Knitting: The Ultimate Knitting Book.* New York: Pantheon Books, 1989.

Newton, Deborah. *Designing Knitwear.* Newtown, CT: Taunton Press, 1992. Reprint, paperback, 1998.

Righetti, Maggie. *Knitting in Plain English.* New York: St. Martin's Press, 1986.

Square, Vicki. *The Knitter's Companion.* Loveland, CO: Interweave Press, 1996.

Stanfield, Lesley, and Melody Griffiths. *Encyclopedia of Knitting: A Step-by-Step Visual Guide, with an Inspirational Gallery of Finished Works.* London: Running Press, 2000.

Stanley, Montse. *Knitter's Handbook: A Comprehensive Guide to the Principles and Techniques of Handknitting.* London: David and Charles, 1986. Reprint, paperback, 1999.

Thomas, Mary. *Mary Thomas' Knitting Book.* London: Hodder and Stoughton, 1938. New York: Dover Publications, reprint, 1972.

Walker, Barbara G. *A Treasury of Knitting Patterns.* Pittsville, WI: Schoolhouse Press, 1998.

Walker, Barbara G. *A Second Treasury of Knitting Patterns.* Pittsville, WI: Schoolhouse Press, 1998.

Zimmermann, Elizabeth. *Elizabeth Zimmermann's Knitters' Almanac.* New York: Dover Publications, 1985.

Zimmermann, Elizabeth. *Elizabeth Zimmermann's Knitting Workshop.* Pittsville, WI: Schoolhouse Press, 1981.

Zimmermann, Elizabeth. *Knitting Without Tears; Basic Techniques and Easy-to-Follow Directions for Garments to Fit All Sizes.* New York: MacMillan Publishing Company, 1973.

Videos

Videos are great for people who are more visual learners.

VICTORIAN VIDEO PRODUCTIONS
(785) 842-1675
FAX (785) 842-0794
crafts@VictorianVid.com

Organizations

Join the club and get together with fellow knitters on a social and educational level. The national guild holds annual conventions and regional conferences with classes and vendors. It also puts out its own magazine. There are local and regional guilds. Contact them to find out if there's a group near you.

THE KNITTING GUILD OF AMERICA®
1100-H Brandywind Blvd.
P.O. Box 3388
Zanesville, OH 43702-3388
(740) 452-4541
(800) 274-6034

tkga@tkga.com
www.tkga.com

THE CRAFT YARN COUNCIL OF AMERICA (CYCA)
P.O. Box 9
Gastonia, NC 28053
(704) 824-7838
FAX (704) 824-0630
cycainfo@aol.com
www.craftyarncouncil.com
www.knitandcrochet.com

This is an industry trade association. In addition to sponsoring an educational program, CYCA acts as a clearing house for the craft yarn industry, when possible answering consumer inquiries and providing links to consumer knitting and crocheting guilds. It sponsors community-based programs such as Warm Up America and Caps for Kids, which keep us in touch with thousands of knitters and crocheters around the country. The Council was formed in 1981 to raise awareness of yarns.